# How far is too far?

I glanced at Melissa, but I had no way to talk to her without Reb and Jennifer hearing us. Maybe she wouldn't even care. We all got into bed, and Tis turned out the lights. Then Melissa made a funny noise. We could hear her kicking her covers around in the dark.

"Melissa, is everything all right over there?" called Reb out in a sugar-sweet tone. I could hear Jennifer snickering from the top bunk.

"Yeah."

"Are you sure? Need me to tuck you in, since Rachel isn't here?"

"No thanks."

"Okay. Just know that if you need anything—I'm here for you."

I felt a little bad. If I'd remembered earlier, I probably would've warned Melissa so she could fix her sheets before lights out. Maybe she didn't even mind that much. I mean, it wasn't *that* big a deal. The way Reb had talked about it, short-sheeting sounded like something really bad, but it was just a little prank.

I wouldn't mind if somebody short-sheeted me. I don't think.

One Summer. One Sleepaway Camp.
Three Thrilling Stories!

How far will Kelly
go to hold on to
her new friends?

What happens when Judith
Ducksworth decides to
become JD at camp?

Can Darcy and
Nicole's friendship
survive the summer?

# Summer Camp Secrets

## PRANKED

### by Katy Grant

**ALADDIN PAPERBACKS**

New York   London   Toronto   Sydney

For my father, Bill Arbuckle,

who has always told me I can do anything I want—

you were right

This book is a work of fiction. Any references to historical events, real people, or real locales are used fictitiously. Other names, characters, places, and incidents are the product of the author's imagination, and any resemblance to actual events or locales or persons, living or dead, is entirely coincidental.

ALADDIN PAPERBACKS
An imprint of Simon & Schuster Children's Publishing Division
1230 Avenue of the Americas, New York, NY 10020
Text copyright © 2008 by Katy Grant
All rights reserved, including the right of reproduction
in whole or in part in any form.
ALADDIN PAPERBACKS, *Summer Camp Secrets*, and
colophon are trademarks of Simon & Schuster, Inc.
Designed by Christopher Grassi
The text of this book was set in Perpetua.
Manufactured in the United States of America
First Aladdin Paperbacks edition April 2008
10 9 8
Library of Congress Control Number 2007935961
ISBN-13: 978-1-4169-3576-6
ISBN-10: 1-4169-3576-2

# Acknowledgments

Many, many thanks to Jen Klonsky, who first read the manuscript for this book way back in 2000, and who sent me the heart-stopping e-mail saying she liked this book and would I be interested in writing a trilogy? Even though the deal did not go through back then, Jen never forgot my camp stories.

Thanks also to my agent, Erin Murphy, who signed me when she was just starting out and who kept me on her list during my long fallow period. Like a good agent should, Erin stayed in touch with Jen over the course of six years and through the birth of two babies, and finally in 2006, the two of them made this happen.

And last, but most important, thanks to my editor, Liesa Abrams, who arrived at Aladdin in fall 2006 and hit the ground running. She hasn't slowed down since.

Where would I be without the three of you? Unpublished—that's where.

## Sunday, June 15

This was definitely going to be the worst summer of my life.

I got out of the car and looked at all the people swarming around. It was mostly parents, but there were some other girls too, and even some brothers who looked as thrilled as I was to be here. Everyone was carrying something, and everyone seemed to know what to do and where to go. Except for us.

I just stood there holding my pillow. Then this woman who seemed to be in charge walked up. She had on a green polo shirt with a little pine tree on it. "I'm Eda Thompson, the camp director. Welcome to Pine Haven!"

My mom smiled with relief, and the two of them

started talking. Dad tried to wink at me, but I acted like I had to scratch my knee.

"This is our daughter, Kelly," my mom said.

"Hi, Kelly." The director smiled at me, then checked her clipboard. "Kelly Hedges, right? And you're twelve?"

I said yes, but it came out all croaky. I cleared my throat. "That's right."

She probably thought I didn't look twelve because I'm so vertically challenged. The director walked over to a group of people wearing green polos just like hers and motioned one of them to follow her back to us.

"This is Rachel Hoffstedder, and she's your counselor." Rachel shook hands with Mom and Dad, and then she shook my hand. She looked okay. She had really short dark brown hair, and she seemed friendly. And she was pretty vertically challenged herself. "Rachel will take you to your cabin." Then the director left to say hello to some other unhappy campers.

"Our cabin's that way." Rachel pointed up a steep hill. I could kind of see some cabins at the top of the hill, hidden in a bunch of trees. My dad was trying to wrestle my new metallic blue trunk out of the back of the car. The website had said we needed trunks to keep all our stuff in because there wasn't any place to store luggage.

"Why don't I get this end?" Rachel grabbed one of the trunk handles before my dad made a complete idiot of himself. Mom had my sleeping bag and tennis racket. I didn't have anything to carry but my pillow, which was better than nothing. At least it gave me something to hold on to.

We passed a bunch of other campers and parents going up the hill. I could tell some of them were really nervous. But then a lot of them acted like old friends. Girls kept shrieking at each other and hugging. It was beyond stupid to watch. I tried to relax my face and look casual, but my heart was pounding so hard I could feel the pulse in my throat.

What was I thinking when I agreed to this? Did they hypnotize me? Was it one of those weird parental mind control things?  How had my parents ever talked me into spending a month at summer camp?

They started talking about camp back in March. They showed me the brochure and the website, and at that time it looked pretty cool. *Camp Pine Haven for Girls, located in the scenic mountains of North Carolina. A camping tradition since 1921.* Anyway, my best friend, Amanda, was going to be in Hawaii for two weeks, lying on a beach surrounded by a hundred gorgeous surfers. I figured she could miss me for two weeks after she got back from her dream vacation. In March camp seemed like a good idea. But that was March.

We walked up a dirt path and came to this big stone building with a porch. "That's Middler Lodge," said Rachel, and then we turned up another path and climbed a bunch of stone steps that went up yet another hill. There sure were lots of hills. My dad tried desperately not to pant, because Rachel wasn't breathing hard at all. She'd told us she was on the hiking staff, so she probably walked about thirty miles a day or something.

By now we were finally at the top of the hill where all the cabins were. There was a really wide dirt path, and all down one side was a long row of cabins. "This is Middler Line, and we're in Cabin 1A. You guys are in the middle between the Juniors—the little kids—and the Seniors—the oldest girls."

Rachel pushed open the screen door of the first cabin we came to, and she and my dad stumbled in and plopped my trunk on the floor. They each took a big breath.

"How many girls in each cabin again?" asked Mom.

"Eight, with two counselors. This is 1A, Kelly, and that's 1B." She waved to the left side of the cabin.

"You're number one! You're number one!" Dad

chanted. I wanted to hit him with my pillow, but I just looked around at everything.

Rachel laughed at his stupid joke, then spread out her arms. "Well, here it is. Your home away from home."

I'd seen the cabins in pictures on the website, but that didn't really give me an accurate view. I wouldn't be surprised if this cabin was built in 1921. It was all gray wood. The top half of the front and back walls were really just screens. The ceiling had wood beams across it with a couple of bare lightbulbs hanging down from them. But the weirdest thing was that there was graffiti *all* over the walls. Everywhere you looked, you could see where someone had written her name. There wasn't a blank space of wall anywhere. The website had called the cabins "rustic." "Primitive" was more like it.

"You're the first one here, so you get your choice of beds. This is mine, of course." Rachel pointed to a made-up cot against the wall. I had my choice of one set of bunk beds or two single cots next to them. They all looked uncomfortable. "The bottom bunk has extra shelf space. That's always a plus."

"Okay." I dropped my pillow on the bed.

"Let's get your bed made," said Mom. Rachel and my dad stood around looking useless, and I wandered toward the other side of the cabin, which was also full of empty bunks. And then I noticed something.

"Ah, excuse me, but . . . where's the bathroom?"

"They're not in the cabins. They're in another building down the line."

"You're kidding." I crossed my arms and glared at my dad. At home we didn't have to hike to the bathroom.

"Oh, it's not that bad." Dad tried not to smile. "It's like a college dorm. Let's see the rest of camp before your mom and I take off."

Just then another counselor and camper came in. Rachel helped them with all the stuff they were carrying. Then she introduced the counselor in 1B, Andrea Tisdale, who she said was a CA—a Counselor Assistant. I'm sure Mom and Dad were glad I didn't get her, because she was, like, in training or something. She said her activity was tennis. She was a lot taller than Rachel, and her long blond hair was in a ponytail.

As we were leaving, Andrea leaned over to Rachel and kind of whispered, "No sign of the Evil Twins yet, huh?"

Rachel laughed and shook her head. *Evil Twins?* What was that supposed to mean? My heart skipped three beats.

Rachel showed us the bathrooms. They were in

a building that looked kind of like the other cabins, except it was larger and had no screens. One side had a bunch of sinks, and the other side had a bunch of stalls. "This is 'Solitary.' And the showers are over there." She pointed to another building across from the bathrooms.

"Solitary?" I asked. I watched a granddaddy longlegs crawl down the wall of one stall.

Rachel smiled. "Yeah, that's what we call the bathrooms at Pine Haven."

"Why?" I mean, seriously. Why not just call it a bathroom?

"I'm not sure. Maybe because you're supposed to be by yourself but it's a communal toilet, so you're not really, or . . ." She just looked at me and shrugged.

Whatever. I know you're supposed to "rough it" at camp and all, but actually giving up private bathrooms, hair dryers, and air-conditioned houses with no crawly things—hey, this wasn't going to be easy. How long was I stuck here for? Four weeks—twenty-eight days. All right. Twenty-eight and counting.

After that Mom and Dad hung out for a while, looking at the camp. New campers were arriving all the time. I kept wondering about the *Evil Twins*. What was that all about? And were they in *my* cabin? The counselors had laughed about it, but that name didn't sound funny to me. I looked at all the strange faces around me. Who were the evil ones?

Then we heard a loud bell ringing—a real bell that a counselor was ringing by pulling a rope to make it clang.

"Lunchtime, Kelly. I'll see you in the dining hall," said Rachel.

Okay, so now my parents had to leave. My heart was beating about two hundred beats a minute. Dad gave me a bear hug and reminded me to write lots of long letters.

"We'll miss you so much!" said Mom. I could tell she was trying not to cry, which made me want to walk off without even saying good-bye.

"I'll be okay." My voice sounded like somebody else's. I hugged Mom really fast and then walked toward the dining hall without looking back. I could barely see it through the blur, but I blinked enough so that none of the tears rolled out.

Okay. So far, so good. I'd managed to say good-bye without crying. Much.

The dining hall had two screen doors, and I got squished by the crowd, all trying to squeeze through at the same time. Inside was a bunch of green wooden tables. I looked around, not sure what to do. I was still blinking really hard, and my nose tingled.

"Kelly, over here!" I saw Rachel and Andrea at a table in the corner, so I wiggled through the mob. On the table was a little white card folded in half with MIDDLER CABIN 1 printed on both sides. I sighed and sat down. At least I wasn't going to have to eat by myself. Four other girls were already at the table. None of them looked evil, but then sometimes you can't tell by looking.

We had tacos and fruit salad, but I had a hard time swallowing, because there was something like a walnut stuck in my throat. I got to meet Jordan, Molly, and Erin, who were all on Side B. Jordan and Molly came together, and they were obviously best friends. They spent the whole time talking about horses. Molly had dark hair and dark eyes, and she was short and squatty, kind of like a fire hydrant. But she seemed more outgoing than Jordan, who was quiet and pretty. There was something about Erin that seemed really grown-up. The only other Side A person was Melissa, and everything about her was pale—pale skin, pale eyes, even pale hair.

"Is this your first year?" Molly asked me, the second after I took a bite of taco.

I chewed fast. "Yeth." I swallowed and tried not to cough.

"It's our second."

That started a conversation about how long everyone had been coming here. Everyone was really impressed that it was Andrea's seventh summer. It seemed like the longer you'd been coming here, the more status you had.

That meant I had no status. No status and no friends. I looked at all these new faces. Did any of them look like friend material? Probably not Molly and Jordan. They had each other, so they didn't need me. Maybe Erin or Melissa. There were three empty chairs for the girls who still weren't here, and two of those chairs were for the Evil Twins. Just thinking about them made me want to heave up my tacos.

After lunch we went back to the cabin for rest hour.

"Okay, ladies—so we all get to know one another, we wear these the first week," said Rachel. Then she and Andrea passed around name tags made out of little circles of wood with a string to hang them around our necks. Andrea's said TIS, which was short for Tisdale. That's what everyone had called her at lunch.

Rachel hung up two name tags on a nail by the door. One said REB; the other said JENNIFER. The wooden circles swung back and forth on the nail and then stopped. I tried not to look at them. At least they didn't say Darth Vader and Lord Voldemort.

"So, Melissa, which bed do you want?" Rachel asked the pale girl.

"The one by the wall, I guess."

From my bottom bunk, I watched her and Rachel make up one of the single cots. After they finished, Melissa sat on her bed and organized her stuff on the shelves. Any time I glanced at her, she looked away. Whatever.

Rachel sat on her bed listening to her iPod and shuffling through papers on her clipboard. She told us that rest hour was the only time we could listen to our MP3 players. We also had to be quiet, which was no problem.

Who was I going to talk to? I held a book in front of my face so I didn't have to stare at all the graffiti.

I must've been out of my mind coming to a camp where I didn't know one single human being. I knew this was a bad idea when Mom started sewing name tags in all my clothes. "What if nobody there likes me?" I'd asked.

Mom had just stared at me as if I'd said something random, like, *What if everyone there secretly turns out to be an extraterrestrial?*

"Now why wouldn't they like you?" she'd replied.

I wished it was that simple. I wasn't used to making new friends. I've always gone to the same school, and I've known all my friends forever. What if I didn't know how to make new ones? Mom made it sound like making friends was no big deal. But obviously lots of girls here already had friends. What if the new girls paired up, like, *today*, and I was a leftover—like the extra odd number when you count off in twos for teams in PE.

A bell rang, which must've meant the end of rest hour, because Rachel put down her clipboard and pulled her earbuds out. She smiled at Melissa and me. "Time for swim tests," she announced, jumping off her cot. "Everybody does it the first day. Get your suits on, ladies, and let's go to the lake!"

I got up and looked through my trunk for my suit.

When I found it, I turned toward the wall, with my back to Melissa and Rachel.

I hated this part. Why was it that some girls never seemed to mind getting naked in front of other people? They always acted really casual, like it was natural to take off your clothes in front of twenty other people. But they were usually the ones with boobs, so they had something to flaunt.

I just barely got a bra this year. And I almost died when I saw the camp application. It had a question that said, "Has your daughter begun menstruating?" My mom had written "No" in the blank. What if my dad had seen that? Why was it their business, anyway?

After we had our suits on, we all walked out together. Molly and Jordan talked to each other about horses, but the rest of us kept quiet. I was so glad we were in a group. I'd die if I had to walk to the lake alone. Then it was obvious you didn't have friends.

As lakes go, this one was really pretty small. I couldn't believe there wasn't a pool. Was it safe to swim in a lake? The water was green, but not slimy green. It looked just like a mirror, the way it reflected the trees and grass. I could see the wet heads of a few girls bobbing up and down in the water, and a couple of counselors stood on a wooden dock, holding clipboards and shouting directions.

A bunch of girls sat on a large, flat rock by the edge of the lake, waiting their turn, so we all sat down too.

"The water's really cold."

I turned around to see who'd said that. It was Melissa, the pale girl.

"Is it?" It was stupid, but it was all I could think of.

"Yeah, it's freezing. The lake water comes from that little stream over there."

"Ugh. I hate swimming in cold water."

"Me too." She sat there, hugging her knees under her chin.

I stared at the edge of the water and noticed some little squiggly things swimming around. "What are those? There's something alive in there!"

"It's just tadpoles," said Melissa.

"Tadpoles?"

"Yeah. They won't hurt you." Then she didn't say anything else. If she hadn't talked to me first, I sure wouldn't have gone out of my way to get to know her.

But at least now I had someone to talk to. It was better than nothing. Besides, I might need some help to ward off any evil influences.

# CHAPTER 3

After the swim tests Melissa and I walked back to the cabin together wrapped in our towels. We were both still shivering, and Melissa's lips were blue. One girl had to be pulled out when she got tired. It was pretty dramatic, and everyone was talking about it. I was so glad something embarrassing like that didn't happen to me.

"So this is your second year?" I asked Melissa.

"Yeah." She shuddered and clutched her towel tighter.

"I guess you know a lot of people then, huh?" Any minute now, Melissa could run into some old friends and hug them, and I'd be all alone again.

"Well, some people are back from last year, but not everyone came back."

"What about the other two Side A girls? Rachel

called them the Evil Twins. Do you know them?" Saying their nickname out loud made me feel like I was calling upon demon spirits.

"Oh, yeah. Reb Callison and Jennifer Lawrence. I can't believe I got into *their* cabin."

"How'd they get that nickname?" My heart was pounding a little, like I'd just asked her to tell me a ghost story.

Melissa bit her bottom lip. "I don't know. Last summer they were sort of . . . wild. You know, during assemblies and stuff."

She watched her flip-flops kick the loose gravel of the road and didn't say anything else. I waited for more information. Did she not want to talk about them?

"Do you wish they weren't in our cabin?" I asked finally.

Melissa looked up. "What I do wish is that Annie Miller was in our cabin. She was supposed to be, till she broke her ankle playing soccer. So now she's going to miss the whole camp session! She was my best friend last summer."

"Wow, that's too bad." Okay, good. It was a relief to know she didn't have a best friend waiting somewhere.

When we got to Middler Line, Melissa stopped in the bathrooms—Solitary, or whatever—and I waited around for a second. Should I wait for her, or would that seem weird? I decided to go to the cabin. I didn't want her to think I was stalking her. But after I left, I wondered if she'd wonder why I didn't wait for her. Maybe I should've just pretended to go to the bathroom too, and timed it so we left together.

When I got to the cabin, there was someone new inside. She was tall and skinny, with bushy, reddish brown hair. Whoever this was, she must be one of the twins. I tried not to make eye contact.

"Hi. Are you in the bottom bunk?"

"Yeah." I wished Melissa would come back from the bathroom. I didn't want to face this twin alone.

But this new girl was busy looking over her choice of beds: the top bunk or the other single between Melissa's and the bunk beds. While she was distracted with that, I rummaged through my trunk for some clothes.

"I'm Jennifer."

"I'm Kelly."

"Is this your first year?"

"Yeah."

"It's my second." See, that whole status thing again. "Do you know if Rebecca Callison is here yet?"

"I'm not sure. A girl named Melissa has that bed."

Her eyes grew two sizes. "Melissa? You mean Melissa Bledsoe?"

"I think so. Blond hair, skinny, kind of quiet . . ."

"Yeah, that's her." Jennifer shook her head and looked at the two empty bunks. I draped my beach towel over me and pulled on jeans and a T-shirt.

"Well, I guess I should take the top bunk. Reb will want the single." She started moving her things. I noticed she had braces, and her eyes were covered by long, shaggy bangs. She honestly didn't seem evil. So far, at least.

When Melissa walked in, she and Jennifer just kind of looked at each other.

Wow, don't everybody talk at once.

"Um, Melissa? Do you want to switch with me? I don't like the top bunk—you know, it's hard to climb up and everything. Do you want it?"

Melissa looked at her, then looked away. I just sat on my bottom bunk and kept quiet. If she asked me to switch, what should I say? I didn't want to switch either.

"You could take that one," Melissa said, meaning the other single cot next to hers.

"Reb will want that one. See, I was thinking, if you'd switch, you two guys"—she turned and nodded at me—"could have the bunk beds and Reb and I could have these singles. Do you mind switching?"

Melissa stared at her bed. "Um, I've already put sheets on."

Just then Rachel walked in and gave Jennifer a big hug.

"So, Jennifer," said Rachel with a smile, "you can have the top bunk or that single one there. What's it gonna be? I'll help you make your bed."

Jennifer looked at Melissa. "So are we going to switch?"

"Uh, no thanks." Melissa looked away and arranged some stuff on her shelf.

Jennifer glared at her. "The top one." Then she and Rachel made up the top bunk, and I sat underneath on my bunk and watched. OMG. I had no idea picking a bed was such an enormous deal. What was up with the two of them? It was a good thing Rachel had walked in.

When her bed was made, Jennifer stood in front of the little mirror nailed to the wall and clenched her teeth together, looking at her braces. Except for the whole bed thing, she seemed pretty normal. So what was evil about her? And what about her missing twin?

"I've only had these two months. Do they look weird?" Jennifer asked the mirror. I wasn't sure who she was talking to. She looked at me.

"Uh, no," I said.

She turned back to the mirror. "Well, I hate them."

Just then a counselor yelled outside the screen window, "Reb Callison! Get out here!"

Jennifer ran out the door. "Alex!" The two of them hugged and screamed. I heard Jennifer tell her Reb wasn't here yet. Then a couple of other girls walked up, and *they* asked about Reb too.

Rachel saw me watching them through the screen and smiled. "Reb's fan club."

I nodded and acted like I had to get something from my trunk. This other girl had a fan club? Great. But what happened to anyone who wasn't a member? I had a sick feeling deep in my stomach. Jennifer wasn't the twin to worry about. It was the other one.

Finally the bell rang for dinner. Without that bell, we'd never know what to do. I was so glad I knew where our table was. Counselors went back and forth to the kitchen with dishes of food and pitchers of this drink everyone called "bug juice."

The last girl from Side B was here—Brittany. She smiled all the time. That was a good sign, so I put her on the potential friend list. Was anyone else doing this too—looking around, checking out possible friends? I felt kind of pathetic. Nobody else looked lonely. But then, I probably didn't either. Little did they know.

Now our table had only one empty chair. Tis passed around plates of chicken, green beans, and mashed potatoes. Rachel tried to get everybody talking. She was telling us about the hikes we could go on.

"Thursday we're going to Angelhair Falls. And there's rock climbing and . . ." All of a sudden, the dining hall's screen doors smacked against the wall so hard that everyone stopped and stared. In the doorway a girl stood looking around at everyone. She was kind of smiling, like she was glad she'd gotten everyone's attention. All I could think was, if that'd happened to me, I'd be having one of the most embarrassing moments of my life right now. But she wasn't the least bit embarrassed.

"Reb! Reb! Over here!" screamed Jennifer.

Wow. So this was Rebecca Callison, the missing Evil Twin.

# 4

At first I had the impression that everyone in the dining hall stopped and called out in perfect unison, "Reb is here!" like in those musicals, when everyone is acting semi-normal, and then all of a sudden they start singing a song together. I know it wasn't quite like that, but it did kind of seem that way.

Several people called out her name, and it took her a while to get to our table, because girls kept stopping her and hugging her. Fan club members, obviously. I chewed a bite of green beans, but I couldn't stop watching her move across the dining hall.

I thought Jennifer was going to jump up on the table and start tap dancing, she was so relieved. "Well, it's about time!" She and Reb shrieked and hugged. Were they old war buddies who'd saved each other's lives or something? Finally Reb sat down at our table, all flushed and excited.

Right away I could tell she was a tomboy. She had on a "Got Game?" T-shirt, and her blond hair was really short, like she couldn't be bothered by a brush. She was only a little taller than me, and she was just as flat-chested. She ran her hands through her hair, then looked at all of us and smiled.

"That was quite an entrance, Rebecca," said Rachel, kind of teasing.

"Glad you liked it, Hoffstedder," she answered in the exact same tone. "And if you call me Rebecca again, I'll be forced to flush your hiking boots down the toilet. With you in them. Hey, Tis. Are you our counselor too?"

"Rachel's your counselor, thank God. I'm on Side B. I came this close to drowning myself in the lake"—Tis held up her fingers to show how close—"when I found out the Evil Twins were in the same cabin with me."

"Ah, that's so sweet!" said Reb. "Are we your worst nightmare?"

Rachel and Tis both laughed. "Absolutely."

Tis gave Reb her plate, and Rachel introduced her to all the new campers. She seemed friendly. She asked us all where we were from. It was weird. Rachel had kind of been in charge of the conversation before, but now Reb took over that spot, because she was the one asking everyone questions. She talked to everyone at the table. Well, except Melissa. But then Melissa wasn't exactly the chatty type.

Reb looked right at me and said, "You're on Side A with us? Cool." I felt a rush of warmth at the compliment.

"I figured I'd be the last one in the cabin to get here. You better have saved me a good bunk," she said to Jennifer.

"Yes, Your Highness. You know I did."

After dinner it was just after sunset, and everything was all shadowy and dim, but I watched Reb walking along with her elbow propped on Jennifer's shoulder. Girls were still coming up to her to say hi. She was laughing and talking, and I couldn't stop watching her. Now that I saw her, I got it. The fan club, all the people coming by—it all made sense. There was just something about her—like a magnet. People watched her and followed her and listened to everything she said. It was like we were all waiting for her to show us what to do.

When the other girls walked away, I heard her say to Jennifer, "Oh my God, this is the worst. I can't believe *she's* in our cabin!" Then they started whispering, so I couldn't hear anything else.

My heart pounded. Did she mean me? Did I have bad breath, body odor, a booger on the end of my nose?

Wait a second. She'd just met me. She couldn't mean me. But then who? I had a feeling she probably meant Melissa. But why? I looked around for Melissa, but I didn't see her in the crowd. I'd been too busy watching Reb and Jennifer.

After dinner we went to evening program and played a bunch of "get acquainted" games in the lodge, and then it was time for bed. Everyone crowded into Solitary to brush their teeth and go to the bathroom. A lot of girls were already in pajama pants and T-shirts. Camp seemed like it was going to be one long sleepover.

Back in the cabin, Jennifer groaned about climbing up to the top bunk. "I hope I don't get on your nerves too bad, climbing up all the time," she said to me.

"Don't worry about it," I told her. I was just glad I got to keep my bottom bunk.

Reb picked up Rachel's clipboard. "Do any of you sleepwalk, snore, wet the bed, or have night terrors? Let me know so I can stuff your mouths with socks, strap you down, and put rubber sheets on your mattress." She stood there looking serious until Rachel walked up behind her and snatched the clipboard away.

"Melissa, any issues we should know about?" asked Reb with her arms crossed. She sounded like a teacher getting onto a student about something.

Melissa let out a nervous little laugh. She looked even paler than usual.

"Get in bed, sweet pea," said Rachel.

Reb just ignored her. "Kelly, I want to formally welcome you to Camp Pine Haven. Let me know if I can do anything to make your stay more pleasant. Camp is truly a swell learning experience for us all."

I couldn't help smiling. "Thanks." I knew she was just showing off, but I was glad she welcomed me. And she remembered my name.

Rachel picked up Reb's pillow off her newly made bed and smacked her with it. "I'm having a night terror. I need to stuff a sock in Reb's mouth so it'll stop."

"Ouch! Camper abuse! Tisdale, help me! Rachel's killing me over here!"

Rachel rolled her eyes. "Reb, give me a break. It's only the first night."

Outside someone yelled, "Lights out!" so Rachel turned off the lights.

What a long day. Had it been only this morning when my parents dropped me off? I turned my face into my pillow, and my sheets still smelled like home. All of a sudden that walnut popped back into my throat. Last night my cat, Cheshire, had slept at the foot of my bed like he always did. Now it felt weird to move my feet around without feeling his warm weight.

Cheshire was probably sleeping in my empty bed right now. And here I was, in this strange bed, hundreds of miles from home, surrounded by two counselors and seven strange girls—two of them potentially evil.

I'd never felt so lonely in my whole life.

# CHAPTER 5

## Wednesday, June 18

"Which activity do you want to go to?" I asked Melissa.

"I don't care. Which activity would *you* like to go to?"

I looked at the list of choices on the paper stapled to the wall by the cabin door. "Well, I could do tennis or canoeing. I wouldn't mind crafts, either. Do you have a preference?"

"Not really. Why don't you pick?" said Melissa.

"How about canoeing?" I asked.

"Well, okay. But I'm not very good at it."

"Then would you rather play tennis or go to crafts?"

"No. Canoeing's fine. Tennis is fine. Or crafts. I really don't care."

I nodded, trying hard not to grab Melissa around the neck and choke her. Melissa was nice—actually too nice. I just wanted her to grow a backbone and pick an activity for a change. But she always let me choose.

Everyone in our cabin had turned out to be okay. Rachel tried really hard to make sure we were all getting used to camp. "Everyone having a good time?" she kept asking. But Tis was hardly ever in our cabin. She mostly hung out with all the other CAs.

Molly and Jordan were best friends. Molly, the one who looked like a fire hydrant, was outgoing and friendly. On the second day she'd held up three books and said, "I've got all these to read this summer. I can't wait!" The weird thing was, they were all about the Titanic, which she was totally obsessed with. Jordan, the pretty one, always seemed stressed about something. She worried about being able to do a jump on her horse this summer.

Erin was serious. She wasn't unfriendly; she just seemed older than the rest of us, like she'd seen and done all this before. Brittany, who was always all smiles, had immediately made friends with a lot of people, even from other cabins.

Then there were the Evil Twins. Every chance I got, I watched them. I still hadn't figured out where their nickname came from. But if anything, they seemed more fun-loving than evil. They were always joking around. I'd thought they were going to be snobs, but they weren't like that at all.

When we had to go to activities for the first time, I watched to see where everyone was going. I wanted to follow Reb and Jennifer, but I lost them in the crowd on the first morning. Melissa was following me and asked if I wanted to go to riflery. Since then we'd kind of been hanging out. It was better than being alone.

On the way to the lake Melissa and I didn't say much. I tried to make conversation at first, but after a while, I got tired of doing all the work. It was a relief to get to the lake and have something to do. Michelle Burns, one of the canoeing counselors, demonstrated a few strokes to all of us standing around the lake edge, and then she let us get into the canoes and try them out. Melissa and I paddled around, but we kept going in circles.

"Use the J stroke!" yelled Michelle. She'd told us that stroke would help us go straight, and the girl in the stern was supposed to do it. That was Melissa.

"I don't think I'm doing this right," she said. Obviously not. I watched a couple of other girls, Chris and Maggie, moving straight as an arrow across the lake. They smiled as they passed us.

"Here, like this." I showed Melissa. "Remember how

Michelle said to turn the paddle so it's like you're writing a *J* in the water?"

"Okay."

But she still couldn't get it right.

"Maybe we should switch places," I suggested.

"Okay. If you think so." Melissa stood up, but that just made the canoe wobble, which made her grab the sides, which made her drop her paddle in the water. She sat down really quickly and leaned over the side to grab her paddle, but that made the canoe tilt over, and she came very close to falling headfirst into the lake.

"Hang on a second. I think I can reach it." With my paddle, I managed to steer us over to where her paddle was floating, and I leaned out and grabbed it. "Here ya go."

"Thanks. I'm sorry I'm so much trouble."

"Don't worry about it."

We spent the rest of the morning spinning around in circles. We almost ran over a couple of swimmers in the middle of a class. I made a mental note to get in the stern next time. Melissa kept apologizing, and I kept telling her it was okay.

I was so glad when morning activities ended. Walking back to the cabin, we ran into Reb and Jennifer leaving the tennis courts. As soon as I saw them, I wished we'd gone to tennis.

"Hi, guys."

"Hi, Kelly," said Jennifer.

"What's up, Kel?" asked Reb. So far they'd both been friendly to me, but they had a way of never acknowledging Melissa's existence. I could tell they didn't like her, but I wasn't sure why. I kind of wished they hadn't seen me with her.

"How was your game?"

"Good game. Good game." Reb balanced the end of her racket on the palm of her hand.

Jennifer bent down to tie her shoelace, and we all stopped. "Yeah, for you it was. For me it was a humiliating defeat. You ought to play Tisdale or the other counselors if you want to improve your game. I'm tired of losing."

"Oh, right. Like I never lose. When I play my brother or my dad, I end up crawling off the court. Talk about humiliation." Reb tossed her racket into the air, caught it, then spun it between her palms. Obviously, she'd never lose her paddle in the water or get stuck in a canoe going in circles.

"My dad has a serve like a cannonball. Once he hit me right here"——she rubbed her shoulder——"and it left a huge bruise that stayed there forever. I told him I didn't want to play him anymore, because I was afraid one of his serves would hit me and I'd die of a hemorrhage. He told me, 'Fear's a good teacher. Gives you an edge.'"

"That's pretty mean." The second I said it, I knew I'd messed up.

"My dad's not mean! You don't even know him! He's a great guy!"

"Uh, no, I meant . . . it just sounds a little . . ." I wanted to hit the backspace and delete that last comment. Too bad real conversations don't work like IMs.

"Hey, if it weren't for my father, I wouldn't even know how to play tennis." Reb frowned at me. "My parents have always helped my brother and me to be the best. They put us in sports, music lessons, art lessons, everything—trying to find out where our talents were. And now my brother Zach just finished his first year at Brown. And I'm going to an Ivy League school too. My parents and I are already making plans."

"Reb, your parents are pretty intense," said Jennifer. "You have to admit."

"What's intense about wanting us to be good at stuff? That's not intense, that's . . . being a good parent."

"Sorry. I didn't mean anything bad about your dad," I said. I hoped Reb wasn't mad at me. Nobody said anything else. All of a sudden Melissa stopped and bent down.

"Oops. Sorry. I hate when that happens," Reb said, and I saw that she'd stepped on the heel of Melissa's sneaker and given her a flat tire.

"That's okay." We all stopped while Melissa wriggled her heel back inside her shoe. Reb sounded sorry, but then I saw Jennifer give her a playful slap.

I felt a little bad for Melissa, but I was so relieved Reb hadn't done that to me. She might have, to get back at me for that comment. Why'd she pick on Melissa, though?

Maybe because Melissa hadn't said a single word. She might as well be invisible sometimes. Sure she was shy, but she could at least *try* to take part in the conversation.

In the cabin I rummaged through my trunk and found my secret bubble gum stash. We weren't supposed to have gum, candy, or snacks in the cabins. Supposedly that stuff would attract ants. A likely story. They probably just said that to scare us. I offered everyone a piece, but Jennifer couldn't because of her braces and Melissa said no thanks. Reb took a piece, and I hoped it made up for my stupid comment.

Melissa stood in the doorway looking at me. "What should we do now, Kelly?"

I plopped down on my bunk and stared up at

Jennifer's bedsprings above me. "Nothing." It was morning free time. We had a half hour before lunch to do whatever we wanted, and I really didn't want to spend it with Melissa.

"Want to go swimming?"

"No, we just came from the lake. I don't feel like walking all the way back."

She just stood there. I was busy blowing bubbles. Reb was organizing her trunk, something she did at least two or three times a day. She hated to have anything out of place. Jennifer was brushing her bushy hair in front of the tiny mirror on the wall. Neither of them said anything.

"I guess I'll take a shower," said Melissa. There was really no good time to take a shower. In the morning we had to get up, clean the cabin for inspection, and go to breakfast, all in thirty minutes. At night we had evening program, and then we had to go straight to bed. You had to find weird times to take showers, like before lunch.

She got her shower stuff and left. Good. When she was out of earshot, Reb burst out laughing. "I thought she was gonna ask you to wash her back or something."

"Gross!" I groaned. "The thought of washing Melissa Bledsoe's pale, skinny back . . ." I made puking noises into my cupped hands, and Reb acted like she was heaving. It was kind of mean, but I'd never say that to her face. Anyway, Reb was right. Melissa had turned into a leech. We didn't have to spend every single minute together.

Jennifer looked at me. "You aren't friends with her, are you?" Her nose wrinkled.

"She's not my BFF, if that's what you're implying. I barely know her." And that was true. Melissa was okay, but she definitely wouldn't have been my first choice as a friend.

"Well, you two have been hanging out a lot. You look pretty chummy to me." Jennifer turned back to the mirror and clenched her teeth. Anytime she looked in the mirror, she made that face.

My stomach tensed up. I was dying to say something. I blew a huge bubble that popped all over my face, then I sucked all the gum back in. "It seems like you guys don't like her much."

Jennifer snorted. "Oh, you noticed that, huh? Didn't you see how obnoxious she was to me about the whole bed thing?"

"Yeah." Although I wouldn't exactly have called Melissa obnoxious.

Reb closed her trunk and plopped down on her bed. "Nobody likes her. It's because of last summer."

"What happened last summer?" Maybe now I could finally find out what was up.

Reb blew a bubble and popped it. Then I blew one. We kept making smacking noises. She was better at it than I was.

"Well, last summer we knew this girl, Heather Crabtree. She was in Melissa's cabin, and she couldn't stand her. She told us all kinds of unbelievable things about her."

"Like what?"

"Well, one time Heather and some other people wanted to short-sheet somebody, so they picked this girl Annie, just as a joke, right?"

I had no idea what she meant by "short-sheeting," but I didn't want to look like a complete idiot, so I nodded like I knew what she was talking about.

"Well, so Annie and Melissa are, like, best friends, and they both went crying to the counselor about being short-sheeted. I'm sorry, but your counselor is not your mommy away from home."

Jennifer sat on top of her trunk and looked at me. I could barely see her eyes through her bangs. "But that's not the worst thing about Melissa. Is it, Reb?"

"Oh, no. The worst . . . the WORST! Are you ready for *this*?" Reb leaned forward like she had this big secret.

I sat up and leaned forward so I wouldn't bump my

head on Jennifer's bed. I couldn't believe they were actually confiding in me, a new camper. It was cool that they felt like they could trust me.

"She used to wet the bed last summer." Reb sat back and looked at me.

I made a face like I didn't believe her. Because I didn't really, but I wasn't about to call her a liar.

Jennifer broke out laughing. "Can you believe that? Heather told us."

"Yeah. Heather said that one time she saw this big wet spot on Melissa's bed and so she goes, 'Hey, Melissa, did you have an accident?' Just teasing her, you know. But Melissa says, 'It's from a swimsuit' or something. Then she got all nervous, and she changed her sheets! Now, if she hadn't wet the bed, why'd she change the sheets?"

"That is too weird," I admitted.

"So now we're stuck with Melissa Bledsoe, a bed-wetting narc, in our cabin. Can you imagine any worse luck?" Reb groaned.

"Well, yeah. It could be worse. It could've been worse for *me*," I said. I'd just thought of a good line. I glanced out the screen window to make sure Melissa wasn't coming back.

"Yeah, how?" Reb asked.

"Jennifer wanted her to take the top bunk." I patted

the bottom of Jennifer's bedsprings. "If she had, then *I'd* be waking up with wet sheets every morning too."

"Disgusting!" Reb shouted. We all burst out laughing.

I didn't really believe that stuff about bed-wetting, and I doubted Reb and Jennifer did either, but it was something to laugh about. I was glad the Evil Twins liked my joke.

A few minutes later Melissa came back from the showers, and Reb and Jennifer tried not to laugh. I acted normal and didn't laugh. I did feel bad for talking about her behind her back. The least I could do now was try to be nice to her. But I'd have to find a way of being nice to her without doing it in front of Reb and Jennifer.

# CHAPTER 6

After rest hour everyone was leaving for activities. Reb was putting on her shoes when she looked at me. "So, Kelly, what activity are you going to now?"

"Uh, I haven't decided." I held my breath for what might come next.

"Jennifer and I are going to the climbing tower with some other people. Want to come with us?" she asked, like it was no big deal, like "Hey, is this Wednesday?"— not knowing that when she asked me, my heart actually did a flip. It was like being picked first for teams.

I shrugged, because if she was going to be casual, so was I. "Uh, sure. That sounds like fun." I started to say, "I haven't been there yet," just to make conversation, but I didn't want to overdo it and look like a geek.

Melissa had walked over to the wall where the activities list was posted. She looked at me really fast, then glanced away. Reb and Jennifer were already at the door. I just wanted to walk out with them and not have to deal with Melissa. I looked at her.

"You could do the climbing tower too." I was a little nervous about asking Melissa. Reb and Jennifer had invited me, and then I'd turned around and asked Melissa without checking with them first. And now I knew for sure how they felt about her.

"Um, I don't know." Melissa stared at the activities list, considering her options.

"Yeah, want to come?" asked Reb in the weirdest tone. It reminded me of how my voice came out whenever I had to get Cheshire into the cat carrier to go to the vet's. Those were the only times he wouldn't come to me when I'd call him. Melissa just shrugged and didn't answer. I guess she didn't trust the cat carrier tone either.

Then the three of us left the cabin. I looked back once to see if Melissa was coming, but she wasn't. We *had* invited her. Anyway, she wasn't a new camper like me. She must have *some* friends from last year. She didn't need me to take care of her. I went to morning activities with her. Did that mean I had to go to afternoon activities with her too?

At the climbing tower Reb introduced me to some other girls—Darcy, Nicole, and Meredith. They were all old campers from last year. Thank God for these name tags so I could keep everyone straight. I wasn't used to meeting people and having to remember names.

"Kelly's in our cabin. It's her first year, but she's cool. She's going to hang out with us," said Reb.

What was cool about me? Whatever it was, I wanted to keep doing it. I'd just been awarded a cool badge and I didn't want to lose it.

I couldn't believe I was actually hanging out with Reb and Jennifer, and I was meeting their friends. All those girls I'd watched on the first day—at the time I didn't like them because they all knew each other, and I was alone. But now things had changed.

The climbing tower was so much fun. It was this huge fifty-foot-tall tower made out of tree trunks tied together. Some parts had netting to climb up, and at the very top there was a ledge to sit on, like a tree house. We had to wear helmets and rappelling harnesses and everything. It was *so* scary. Most of us got only about halfway up. Reb was goofing around, driving Rachel crazy. She kept acting like she was falling. We had a blast. I wondered what activity Melissa ended up going to, but it couldn't have been as fun as this one.

By the end of the day it was like I'd been hanging out with Reb and Jennifer and their friends forever. At first I kind of felt like I was holding my breath all the time. I didn't want to have another slip-up and make some stupid remark again. Also, I kept trying to think of funny things to say. Reb was really funny. Jennifer could be too, but mostly she just laughed at things Reb said. It was kind of exhausting having to be funny and careful all the time, but I knew I could do it.

Before evening program we all changed into jeans because it got really cool at night in the mountains, even in summer. I put on a sweatshirt. Reb was wearing a hoodie from Brown. I guess her brother gave her that.

When we walked into the lodge, everyone looked over and called out to us. At least it seemed that way. Reb picked out a long wooden bench for us to sit on. "Hey, Jordan, Molly. Come sit here. This is Cabin One's bench," she called. Then Melissa came in and looked at us, but there wasn't enough room. I mean, there really wasn't. The five of us could barely all squeeze on there. Melissa looked around and found a spot on the floor. Anyway, it wasn't the whole cabin. Erin and Brittany were already sitting on the floor when we came in.

Evening programs were always fun. All the Middlers were together, and we always did something like skits or games. Tonight none of the counselors were inside. The doors to the porch were closed and we could hear them rustling around out there.

Finally the doors opened, and Gloria Mendoza, a counselor in Cabin 4, came out and announced, "Presenting 'The Twelve Years of Pine Haven'!" Then a counselor named Jamie came through the doors. She and Tis were best friends. Her hair was in pigtails, and she was holding a teddy bear. To the tune of "The Twelve Days of Christmas," she sang, "My first year at Pine Haven my mother said to me, 'Don't wet the bed!'"

Reb, Jennifer, and I burst out laughing. We weren't actually laughing *at* Melissa. It was just the bed-wetting joke that made us laugh.

The whole skit was really funny. The counselors made complete fools of themselves, but you could tell they were having a great time. Rachel's line was "Don't eat a newt!" Every time she sang it, she held up a jar with a squiggly orange salamander inside. Tis had one of the funniest lines. She came out with only a towel on and sang, "Don't go skinny-dipping!" Reb kept whistling on her line. She could whistle with two fingers in her mouth. She tried to show me how, but I couldn't do it.

After the skit we were out on the porch, sitting on the upper railing with Alex and some other counselors.

She'd been Reb and Jennifer's counselor last year.

"So, my little Evil Twins are in the same cabin again this year, huh?" asked Alex. "At least *I* don't have to deal with you. You can drive Rachel crazy this summer."

"You know you miss us. You know you love us," said Reb. She stood in front of Alex and pretended to box with her.

Alex grinned. "I'm glad I don't have to put up with your evilness."

"What's evil about them?" I asked as casually as I could.

"Oh, Alex always called us that last summer. *The Evil Twins!*" Reb said in a voice like someone possessed.

"Because you were. You were always together and you were both troublemakers. Always talking too loud. Always the last two out of bed in the mornings. Always laughing and never being serious about anything," said Alex, smiling at them.

"Hey, it's camp. Why should we be serious?" Reb said.

*So that was it?* That was all there was to the "Evil Twins" nickname? Their counselor called them evil because they slept late and talked too much? I felt like a complete idiot. Why had I been so worried?

"So, are you two going to sign up for my Guard Start class?" asked Alex.

Reb glanced at me. "Maybe we'll all three sign up. What is it?"

"It's the first step toward being a lifeguard. You guys are too young to take a lifeguard class, but you can take this class."

Jennifer winced. "Do we have to swim laps? You know I hate that."

"Of course you have to swim laps, Bird Legs. It's a swimming class," said Alex.

"Don't call me Bird Legs. You're mean, Alex." Jennifer frowned and looked down at her long, skinny legs.

"Yeah, don't call my twin names, you Evil Counselor," said Reb. "*Maybe* we'll take your class. But maybe we won't."

Alex just laughed. It was obvious Reb was her favorite.

After evening program we were all walking along, just talking and stuff, when I realized Melissa was right beside us. I hadn't even known she was there.

"Gosh, there are so many stars out tonight," she said. She tilted her head back and gazed up at the sky. I looked up too.

"Wow, there are. There's a ton of them." I'd actually never seen that many stars. The sky was so black in the mountains, and you could see the stars so much better because there weren't many lights around.

"They're bee-yoo-tee-ful," said Reb.

"Yes, simply loverly," agreed Jennifer.

Now I had to say something funny. So I leaned over to Reb and sang softly, "Tinkle, tinkle little star, how I wonder what you are." Reb snorted and poked me in the ribs. Jennifer started singing it too, but louder.

Okay, it was a little mean. But I didn't think Melissa heard the "tinkle, tinkle" part.

It was crazy in the cabin before lights out, as usual. On Side B, Brittany screamed when a spider crawled down the wall. Tis picked up one of Jordan's riding boots to kill it, but Jordan shouted that she didn't want squashed spider guts all over her boots. Erin got it into the dustpan and threw it out the door. If there was ever a problem, Erin was always the one to take care of it.

All of us on Side A had stopped to watch the drama. Molly said maybe the spider had laid eggs, and pretty soon a zillion little spiders would hatch out and infest our trunks. That made everyone scream again, especially Jordan, who now had something new to stress about.

Then Rachel flashed the lights on and off as a warning. "Lights out in two minutes. Everybody in bed." It was her serious counselor voice.

"I just have one quick announcement to make," Reb said, leaping up on her cot so everybody on Side B could see her too. "Please don't anyone leave any wet swimsuits on my cot. I hate it when that happens." She bounced down on her knees like you do on a trampoline.

Jennifer and I both laughed. Everybody else looked confused.

Rachel gave her this long look like she suspected Reb was up to something. "Good point, Reb. Let's all be *courteous* and *kind* to one another. It'll make for a more pleasant camping experience."

"Rachel, with you as our counselor, how could our camping experience be anything but pleasant?" Reb said sweetly.

"Uh-huh." Rachel flipped off the lights.

Reb started singing very softly, "Tinkle, tinkle, little camper, can your sheets get any damper. . . ."

"Reb!" Rachel's voice had a warning in it.

"Hey, I'm singing myself a lullaby. It's hard to fall asleep without my mommy."

"I'm gonna write your mommy and tell her you're an 'obnoxious, disruptive influence in the cabin.'"

"She'll be so proud."

"Just tone it down."

"You betcha, Raych. Hey, can I have a night-night kiss?"

"You mean from my newt?"

"Of course! You didn't think I meant *you*, did you?"

I couldn't help laughing. Wow, what a great day. I'd met a bunch of new people, and I'd had so much fun with them. Amazingly, my mom had been right. I did just sort of make friends without even knowing it was happening.

Was I mean to Melissa? Well, we did ask her to go to the climbing tower with us. She chose not to. We couldn't force her to go along. The tinkle, tinkle stuff was a little mean, but it was just a joke. I doubted she'd even heard it.

Anyway, what was I supposed to do? Turn down Reb and Jennifer and spend the afternoon trying to drag a conversation out of Melissa? She'd be okay. She could find her own friends. That's what I'd done. It just took me a few days to do it.

# CHAPTER 7

## Friday, June 20

"Run! Here it comes!" Reb yelled. We raced down Middler Line, trying to beat the rain. We got to the screen door just when the first raindrops started falling.

"Wow, listen to it," I said. The cabin had a tin roof, and it sounded like BBs hitting a pie pan.

"I can't believe we're the only ones here," said Jennifer. "You'd think everyone would be cabin-sitting in this rain."

"Probably most people got caught some place like the lodge," Reb speculated. She and Jennifer both sat on their trunks, and I was on my bottom bunk. It was fun always having a big group to hang around with, being part of the fan club, but I liked it best when it was just the three of us.

Jennifer looked at us both. "What should we do?"

Reb's eyes widened. "Let's tell ghost stories!"

"I'm not in the mood." Jennifer shook her head.

"You mean you're scared."

"How could I be scared? You haven't said anything yet."

"Okay, good. I'll start. This is a true story, Kelly. Alex told it to us last summer. Have you ever heard of the Bell Witch?"

"No, Reb! Shut up!" Jennifer jumped up and grabbed her pillow from the top bunk. "You know how much that one scared me!" She stuck her fingers in her ears, buried her face in the pillow, and started humming. "I'm not listening!"

Reb burst out laughing. "I was just teasing. You know I wouldn't really tell it."

Jennifer hugged her pillow. "Still, you reminded me of it, and that's bad enough."

"Okay, sorry. Let's do something to take your mind off it."

"How about cards?"

"Bor-ing. Kelly, what do you want to do?"

I kind of smiled. "Why don't you read us the e-mail you got today?"

I could tell Reb was glad I'd brought it up.

Everyone in the cabin knew she'd gotten an e-mail from her boyfriend back home. "Well, okay." She jumped up and opened her trunk to get the paper. Mail came every day after lunch. Whenever anyone got an e-mail, the counselors printed the message and put it in the camper's mailbox. But we could only get e-mails, not send them, because campers weren't allowed to use the computer in the camp office.

Reb read, "'Yo, Reb! What up, chica? Hope you're having fun at camp, 'cause it's sure boring round here. So what have you been doing? I went to Big Surf with Mikey on Tuesday. We saw Lindz and Brittney. Got to go. Have fun, but not too much. Try not to miss me too much. Later. Bye. Wes.'"

Reb looked up and grinned. Okay, it wasn't wildly romantic, but at least he wrote her, and first.

Jennifer got up and stood in front of the mirror. "Pretty good letter."

"I guess," Reb agreed. "But he's trying to make me jealous, mentioning Lindsay. She's always liked Wes. She's probably chasing him while I'm at camp."

"Really?" Jennifer squinted at her reflection. "You oughta write her and tell her to keep her hands off your boyfriend."

Reb shrugged. "Well, if Wes and I break up, I'll

start going out with Daniel Cook. He's liked me since fifth grade. I thought Wes would want to break up since I was going to camp, but he didn't. He must really like me. Wanna see his picture?" She grabbed her school annual from the shelf by her bed.

Then she showed us every place Wes Mitchell appeared in the annual. He and Reb were in there a lot—they were both on the soccer and swim teams, plus Reb was on the tennis team. Reb was the class president and Wes was the treasurer. And they were both on the annual staff, except her school called it the yearbook staff. There was a picture of the two of them sitting at a table together. It looked like they were making vital decisions about which pictures to put where.

Wes was drop-dead gorgeous—the kind of guy who always made me speechless. Of course Reb would have a bf like that.

"You've got so many cute guys in your school," Jennifer said, looking at all the pictures. "I hate going to a girls' school. And wearing a uniform. And going to Mass."

"My parents thought about sending me to a girls' school too, but we decided Country Day was giving me the best preparation for college."

Jennifer rolled her eyes. "Reb, shut up. You're only

going into seventh grade. I can't believe how obsessed you and your parents are with college already. They can't even leave you alone at camp."

It was true. Reb's parents e-mailed her math problems to work on and vocabulary words to study. Every rest hour, she sat on her cot with a pad of paper in her lap and a pencil clenched between her teeth. I thought it was weird, but Reb didn't seem to mind.

"We're not obsessed with it. We're just preparing, that's all. And why are you always criticizing my parents? If it weren't for them . . ."

"I know, I know. If it weren't for them riding you all the time, you wouldn't be perfect. But you are perfect, so you'd think they'd get off your back and just let you be a kid. I thought *my* parents were tough."

Reb slammed her annual shut and threw it at the shelf. It banged against the wall and fell to the floor. We all stared at it, like we didn't know how it got there. None of us moved. The rain drummed against the roof.

I don't know how I knew what to say, but somehow I did. I looked at Reb and said, "Wow. Nice serve."

Reb looked at me and burst out laughing. "Thanks. Fifteen-love. Your service."

Jennifer and I were both laughing now too. "I can't serve like that!" I said.

"Well, of course you can't, because you're not *perfect* like me, now are you?" asked Reb, laughing. She screwed up her face and snarled at Jennifer, who snarled back.

I let out a shuddering laugh. "Well, if we're not going to play tennis, what are we going to do? We have the whole cabin to ourselves." I was so relieved we were laughing now. It could've gotten ugly.

Reb stood up and looked out the screen door at the rain. Then she looked at us with a sly grin. "I know what we can do. Let's short-sheet Melissa."

# CHAPTER 8

Jennifer actually squealed when Reb said that. "Why didn't we think of that a long time ago?"

Great. I'd barely recovered from the book-throwing incident. Jennifer and Reb rushed over to Melissa's bed. I picked up Reb's annual and put it back on the shelf. It'd been such a relief—somehow I'd been the one to make things right again. Maybe because Reb was always making jokes. I'd managed to make her laugh, and everything was fine.

But now this. It'd been days since we'd joked about the bed-wetting. We'd just left Melissa alone. What was short-sheeting, anyway? When Reb had mentioned it before, she'd just assumed I knew what she was talking about. But no way could I ask them.

"Hold on. Somebody ought to be lookout," Reb said.

"I'll do it." Hey, this was my chance. I could be lookout but still watch them.

Reb plopped down on Melissa's bunk like it was her own. It made me feel weird, because there's, like, this unwritten rule that nobody ever sits on anybody else's bed unless they ask you to, like to play cards or something. Reb was looking at all of Melissa's stuff on the wooden shelf by her bed. "Oh, how precious." She held up a stack of paper. "It says 'Melissa.'" Somebody, probably her dad, had made a border and printed up a bunch of blank sheets with her name on it. "Should say 'Dweeb.'" Then Reb stood up and smoothed out the wrinkles she'd left on Melissa's blanket.

"I can't believe we've been here a week, and we're just now short-sheeting Melissa. How inefficient of us!" Reb said with a smile.

She rolled back Melissa's blanket from the foot of the bed and then stopped all of a sudden. "I just thought of something," she said, all dramatic, looking at Jennifer. "What if she wet the bed last night?"

She and Jennifer both shrieked and clutched each other and then broke up laughing.

"Hey, c'mon," I called from the doorway. "Hurry up before someone catches us." I kept glancing out the door. Melissa might show up. Or Rachel. Then what would happen?

Reb and Jennifer got serious. They were unfolding, refolding, and tucking in Melissa's sheets. While I watched them, it hit me. Oh, *short*-sheeting! At the foot of Melissa's bunk, they folded her top sheet so it made a kind of pocket under the blanket. When Melissa got in, her feet would only go halfway to the end of the bed. Was that all there was to it? I thought it was something really bad.

I felt like an idiot for not figuring it out on my own. Well, at least now I knew.

When they got the bed made, they stepped back to admire their work.

"Now let's get out of here!" Reb shouted.

We grabbed rain jackets and ponchos, then took off running down the line. At least we were out of there. And we hadn't been caught. And it wasn't *that* bad.

It was still raining pretty steadily, and we had to jump over all the puddles because Middler Line is just a dirt path, but now it was a muddy, wet mess. We ran down the hill in the slippery, wet grass and stopped under some tall shade trees for cover.

"Where is everybody?" I asked. The whole camp felt deserted. But everything was beautiful in the rain. The grass and leaves were green, and the tree trunks were black, and the whole camp was misty and wet. It made me shiver.

All of a sudden I jumped up and grabbed one of the branches hanging right over our heads and shook it as hard as I could. All the raindrops on the branch came showering down on us. It was like our own little private rain shower. Reb and Jennifer just stood there, frozen. I had no idea what would happen next. Then Reb snapped out of it.

"You are gonna die!" Thank God she had a huge smile on her face. She dove right at me, and I screamed and ran out from under the tree. She chased me all the way down the hill, with me screaming the whole way. Jennifer was still standing under the tree.

"Jennifer, help! Help!" I yelled.

"I'm not gonna help you! I'm gonna kill you too!" Then they both caught me, and Reb dragged me toward this huge mud puddle. I was trying to get away, but the grass was so slippery. Plus I was laughing so hard I could barely stand up.

Reb pushed me right smack down into that mud puddle, and I felt the water seep all the way through to my skin. The whole seat of my jeans was absolutely soaked. I tried to stand up, but Reb had both her hands on my shoulders, holding me down.

"Ah, revenge is sweet!" She laughed evilly. "I AM your worst nightmare!"

"My butt's freezing! Let me up!" I shouted.

Reb looked over her shoulder at Jennifer. "Look who's amazingly dry," she whispered to me. "On the count of three—one, two . . ."

On three I jumped up and we both lunged at Jennifer and dragged her to the mud puddle. After Jennifer got dunked, we both turned on Reb, and by then we'd pulled off our jackets and ponchos, and we started puddle-hopping. When we got tired of splashing, we scooped the mud out of the bottom of the puddles and threw it at each other. It was amazing!

At first none of us aimed that well because we were laughing so hard. But then it was like we were psychic, and Reb and I wouldn't even have to say anything, we'd just look at each other and bombard Jennifer. Then they'd look at each other and trash me! Then Jennifer and I got Reb, and we got her good. The only part of her face not covered in mud was her eyes.

"I have never been this dirty in my *life*!" Jennifer yelled. "Is it in my hair?"

"In your hair, your ears, your nose . . . ," I said.

"Whose idea was this?" asked Reb, then threw one last mud pie in my direction but missed.

Now it had pretty much stopped raining, and people were coming out of hiding. Everybody stared at us and shook their heads like they couldn't believe it. I couldn't believe it either. Every inch of us was covered in mud. I was shivering like crazy. My wet, muddy clothes felt like they weighed a ton.

We went back to the cabin, with people staring at us all along the way. Jennifer got to the door first, and she was walking in when Rachel saw us. "Hold it right there!" She came to the door with Erin and Brittany, and the three of them stared at us with their mouths open.

Rachel shook her head. "You all can't come inside like that."

"What are we supposed to do?" yelled Jennifer.

"Go straight to the showers." Rachel made Brittany and Erin get us towels and dry clothes from our trunks. "And I would suggest showering with your clothes *on* first." Rachel handed us our stuff, trying not to touch us.

We laughed, but it was a pretty good idea, so we did what she said. We got into the showers with all our clothes on and washed the mud off; then we undressed and finished showering. My wet clothes felt like they weighed about twenty pounds when I took them off and hung them over the shower door.

We kept laughing and talking across the shower stalls. The water was so hot that it burned. I wanted to stand there in the water and steam forever.

We were friends. We really were. I'd been holding my breath all week, waiting for Reb and Jennifer to find out I wasn't really cool. But maybe I *was* cool.

# CHAPTER 9

That night after evening program, we were leaving the lodge when Reb whispered to us, "We're not going to the cabin yet. Keep quiet and follow me."

We could barely see because none of us had flashlights. Crickets were chirping like crazy. The grass was still wet from the rain, and pretty soon my sneakers were soaked. The air was a lot cooler now, and it was really damp. I could smell the wet grass.

"Reb, what's up?" Jennifer sounded annoyed since Reb wouldn't tell us anything.

"We're going to the dining hall for seconds on dessert."

"You mean we're raiding the kitchen?" Jennifer asked. Even in the dark I could hear the nervousness in her voice. Reb would be brave enough to try it, but I was with Jennifer. I was afraid we'd get caught.

"Of course not. Alex is doing it for us."

The kitchen was always open to the counselors. They could go in and help themselves to leftovers whenever they wanted. But they never gave us anything. How had Reb talked Alex into this?

"We're supposed to be in the cabin by now," Jennifer said. I was glad she'd said it because it's what I was thinking.

"Calm down. Rachel has line duty tonight, so she won't even miss us."

At the dining hall we went around back to a screen door. We could hear counselors talking inside. Pretty soon a shadow came out of the kitchen door.

"Reb?" came a loud whisper.

"Alex, over here," Reb whispered back.

Alex clicked on a flashlight and walked toward us. She was balancing two plastic bowls of chocolate pudding in one hand.

"You only brought two?" asked Reb.

Alex looked at me, then back at Reb. "Don't complain. You're lucky to get anything."

Reb gave Jennifer and me the pudding. "You all eat it. I'm not that hungry."

"No, Reb, that's okay." I tried to hand my bowl back to her. Obviously Alex hadn't been expecting me to come along. Reb and Jennifer were her favorite campers from last summer, and she still gave her twins lots of attention.

"Don't be a goof." Reb sounded annoyed. "Go ahead and take it, I don't care."

"We could at least split it."

"So I heard the Evil Twins were out making mud pies in the rain this afternoon."

Jennifer laughed. "Making mud pies of ourselves, you mean."

"Yeah," Reb said around a mouthful of pudding. "Kelly was there too. You know Kelly." Reb said it like Alex and I just needed to be reintroduced. "She's the one who started it all."

"Me?" I acted all innocent. "*You* were the one who threw me into the mud puddle."

"Which I never would have done if you hadn't shaken that branch and gotten us all soaked when we were *trying* to stay dry." She looked at Alex. "Talk about evil! This girl is the worst!"

Alex gave me a look that was a little friendlier. "Too bad I missed it."

"Yeah. We need a new name. We're triplets now."

Reb winked at me and handed me the bowl. I took it like it was a prize.

"Evil Triplets?" asked Alex.

Reb looked thoughtful. "No. Terrible Triplets."

I took a bite of pudding and handed the bowl back to Reb. I was glad it was dark. I had a stupid grin on my face.

"So—I haven't seen you guys in my Guard Start class."

"I know," Reb said. "I guess we're going to be lazy bums this summer." The thing was, we'd talked about the class after Alex mentioned it, but Jennifer didn't want to do it because she wasn't a very good swimmer. Reb was a good friend, though, not letting Alex know that part. Reb gave Alex our empty bowls. "Thanks, Allie. You're the coolest counselor in camp."

We rushed back to the cabin, since we were already late. "Oh my gosh!" Jennifer gasped. "We almost forgot! Melissa's bed!"

"Oh yeah!" said Reb. "We can't miss this!"

I'd actually completely forgotten about short-sheeting Melissa, after the whole mud fight. What if she was really upset? What if she thought I helped them? I didn't really. I just happened to be in the same room with them at the time.

"Where have you all been?" Tis asked when we came in the door.

Reb just shrugged. "We had places to go, people to see."

Tis looked at us. "Really? Care to elaborate?"

"I left my jacket in the lodge, and they went back with me to find it," I blurted out. Reb gave me a quick wink.

Molly looked over from Side B and called out, "Don't believe the Evil Twins, Tis! They were up to something devious."

"Molly, the lifeboats are leaving without you," yelled Reb. Molly drove us all crazy with her weird facts about the Titanic. "Oh, and Evil Twins? That is so last year. Nobody calls us that anymore."

I glanced at Melissa, but I had no way to talk to her without Reb and Jennifer hearing us. Maybe she wouldn't even care. We all got into bed, and Tis turned out the lights. Then Melissa made a funny noise. We could hear her kicking her covers around in the dark.

"Melissa, is everything all right over there?" called out Reb in a sugar-sweet tone. I could hear Jennifer snickering from the top bunk.

"Yeah."

"Are you sure? Need me to tuck you in, since Rachel isn't here?"

"No thanks."

"Okay. Just know that if you need anything—I'm here for you."

I felt a little bad. If I'd remembered earlier, I probably would've warned Melissa so she could fix her sheets before lights out. Maybe she didn't even mind that much. I mean, it wasn't *that* big a deal. The way Reb had talked about it, short-sheeting sounded like something really bad, but it was just a little prank.

I wouldn't mind if somebody short-sheeted me. I don't think.

*Evil Twins—that is so last year.*

I was a triplet now. Could my life get any better?

# CHAPTER 10

## Saturday, June 21

"No way am I wasting my time going to activities!" said Jennifer. Even though Rachel and Tis warned us all about no cabin-sitting, almost everyone was ditching activities to get ready for the dance with Camp Crockett. If there even *was* a dance. We still didn't know for sure, since there hadn't been an official announcement.

Reb just laughed. "I can't believe how stupid everyone's being. You think you'll meet some guy tonight and start a major, long-distance relationship? Please." She looked at me. "Want to go to archery? It won't take *all* afternoon to get ready."

I nodded. "Sure." If Reb wanted to go to archery, so did I.

Jennifer grabbed her robe and towel. "Well, it may

♥ 69 ♥

sound pathetic, but these dances are practically the highlight of my summer. I'm going to meet someone tonight. And I have to look incredible. So I'll see you guys later."

I was surprised she wasn't coming with us, but I was kind of glad it was just Reb and me. On the way to the archery range, I asked Reb, "Why don't the counselors just tell us if there's a dance?" All day they'd acted like it was some big secret.

"So we don't do what Jennifer's doing. Cut activities to get ready," Reb explained. "Jennifer's boy crazy. Going to an all-girls school does that to her."

I thought maybe we'd run into Darcy or Nicole or some of the other girls, but we didn't. Except for the archery counselor watching us, Reb and I had the whole range to ourselves, which was cool. But when we got back to Middler Line late in the afternoon, it was a madhouse. Every single shower had a line of about four or five people waiting.

Devon Fairchild came out of one stall. "There is not a single ounce of hot water left," she announced through clenched teeth, and everyone groaned.

"Reb, we screwed up. We should've stayed with Jennifer. Now we've got to wait in line an hour to get a cold shower," I said.

Reb swung her arm around my neck and gave me this sly grin. "We're not waiting in line for a shower. I know where there's no waiting, and still plenty of hot water."

I just looked at her but didn't say anything. We got our soap and shampoo and put on robes. We walked down Middler Line past the showers and just kept going. Then we went across the hill toward Junior Line. I smiled when I saw where we were heading.

"The Juniors don't get to go to dances, so they'll all be at activities now. Besides, those grubby little rugrats only take about two showers all summer, anyway."

She opened one of the shower stalls and turned on the faucet. Then she stuck her hand into the water and smiled at me. "Warm as bathwater."

"You are a freaking genius!"

She laughed. "I know."

So not only did we both get a hot shower, we didn't have to stand in line. Before I met Reb, I would've just been one of those girls waiting her turn. It was so cool to be friends with someone who knew how to get things done. Plus, all afternoon it'd just been the two of us, Reb and me, without Jennifer or the rest of the fan club. We'd had a great time together.

I wasn't trying to take Jennifer's place, but

sometimes I felt like Reb and I had more in common. We were both more tomboyish, for one thing. I wasn't as athletic as Reb, but I was better at stuff than Jennifer, and I thought Reb admired me for that.

Everybody was in the cabin when we got back. On Side B, Molly was doing Jordan's hair, and even Melissa was putting mascara on her pale eyelashes. Jordan's older sister, Madison, came by and warned us, "You guys better be good. The CATs will be on Porch Patrol." I had no idea what that meant. The CATs were the Counselor Assistants in Training, and Madison was one of them. They were sixteen, and they had the perfect arrangement. They were too old to be campers and get bossed around, but too young to be counselors and have responsibilities, so they could do whatever they wanted.

"It's about time you all showed up!" Jennifer yelled at us. "I'm having a wardrobe crisis! You guys have to help me." She pointed to three outfits spread out on Reb's bed. "Which do you like best?"

"The denim skirt and the pink tank," Reb advised.

"Yeah, I agree. But now what am I going to wear?" I was looking through my trunk. I just didn't pack that many nice clothes.

"Here, you can wear this." Reb pulled out a rose-colored shirt from her trunk and handed it to me. "This will look good with your dark hair."

I almost drooled all over the Abercrombie shirt.

"Don't you want to wear this?" I asked.

"Nah, I'll wear this one." She held up a pale blue Abercrombie polo. "You can borrow some jeans, too, but they might be a little long. I'm wearing my cargos."

"Oh, well, thanks, but I'll wear my jeans." I have one and *only* one pair of Abercrombie jeans. "But thanks for the shirt. It'll look great."

"I wish I was your size." Jennifer looked at us both and grimaced.

"Oh, please. You'd trade those big twins in to be *our* size?" asked Reb.

Jennifer crossed her arms over her chest. "Are they too big? Do they look freakish?"

Reb burst out laughing. "Jennifer, try to find one guy on the planet who would say, 'Hmmm, her breasts are simply too large. I find them freakish.'"

"God, I should've been dieting this week! I knew the dance was coming up!"

"Shut up!" Reb and I both yelled at the same time. Jennifer is the last person in the cabin who needs to diet. I can't believe how weird some girls get about food.

 73

I stood in front of the tiny mirror, trying to see how I looked in Reb's shirt. Practically everything she owned had a moose on it. I had to go through massive amounts of pain and suffering just to get my one little measly pair of Abercrombie jeans.

I first asked my mom for them back in the fall. But when she saw the price tag, she almost had a seizure right there in the mall. "Absolutely not!"

So I asked for them for Christmas. That was *all* I asked for too. If they were so ridiculously expensive, maybe they should be my one and only Christmas present. When Christmas morning came, I got the jeans, but I could tell Mom wasn't happy about having to give in. She gave me this long lecture about the value of a dollar and not being fooled by designer labels, but while I sat there and nodded, I was wearing my new jeans.

"Thanks again for the shirt. I'll be really careful with it."

"Don't worry about it. You can have it if you want it."

"Oh, no! I couldn't *take* it. I'll just borrow it," I said.

"Kelly, it's a shirt. It's not like I'm giving you a kidney." She turned away, acting like it was no big deal. I could tell I'd embarrassed her by drooling over the shirt.

"Here. We should wear these so we'll be triplets." Jennifer handed Reb and me matching pink wristbands.

"At St. Cecilia's, since we wear uniforms, the hip girls all do something different to stand out. Like one day it's striped scrunchies in our hair. Or we all wear blue socks a certain way—you know, rolled down like a dough-nut or just slouched. We have to sneak around the dress code since we can't wear much jewelry. You can tell who's hip and who's not by how they're accessorized."

"What cause is this? Breast cancer?" Reb asked.

"No. Our school had them made. They say St. Cecilia's, but look—I turned them inside out and wrote 'Terrible Triplets' on the other side."

Reb rolled her eyes. "Whatever." But she did put on the wristband to make Jennifer happy. I put mine on because I loved being a triplet.

By dinnertime there still hadn't been an official announcement about the dance, but everyone was all dressed up. We were having spaghetti and garlic bread, and all the old campers said that was a sure sign there was a dance. The garlic bread was supposed to be a joke—nobody would get kissed with breath smelling like garlic. None of us ate any of it.

Jordan pointed out that all the CATs were missing from their table in the center of the dining hall. Then all of a sudden, they burst through the dining room doors. They were all dressed in camo, carrying flashlights, and some of them even had branches and leaves taped to their shirts.

"Ladies and . . . ladies! We know you've been anxiously awaiting an opportunity to see some guys of the male persuasion!" When they said that, we all screamed. "Well, your wait is almost over!" they shouted. "Tonight we'll be going to Camp Crockett for an evening of song and dance!" The noise was earsplitting!

"But be careful! If those Crockett boys want you to sneak away to the bushes for a make-out session, we'll be watching to make sure that nobody leaves the dining hall porch!" Then they all started singing.

> *Porch Patrol! Porch Patrol!*
> *Start yellin' for that good ole porch patrol!*
> *If he tries to make first base, you had better slap his face,*
> *And start yellin' for that good ole porch patrol!*

So now it was official. In thirty minutes we'd be leaving to go to Camp Crockett for Boys.

# CHAPTER 11

They took us over in a bunch of vans and trucks. The dance was in Camp Crockett's dining hall, so all the tables and chairs had been moved to make space for dancing. We walked in, and all of us girls stood clumped together by the door. The boys were way over on the other side of the dining hall. Most of them weren't even looking at us. They were laughing and talking and acting like they were all just hanging out in their dining hall for no reason. There was a huge empty stretch of floor between the boys and us, practically the size of the Grand Canyon. How would anyone ever walk across that big empty space to get to the other side?

I could tell right away that none of *them* had spent all afternoon getting ready for this major event. I suppose they went to the trouble of taking showers. Maybe some of them had even put on clean shirts. To think we put all that energy into looking nice for these boneheads.

"I see three, maybe four guys I could dance with without throwing up," said Reb.

"Well, I'm not wasting any time," Jennifer said. "I say, 'See and be seen.'" She pushed to the front of the group of girls, where she'd be more visible. As we stood there, a few people started to dance. Reb kept making sarcastic remarks until a boy walked up and asked her to dance.

"Sure, why not?" Miss Casual. So now both Reb and Jennifer were dancing, and I was by myself. I was about to go find Erin or Brittany or one of the fan club girls when I turned around and almost fell over a boy.

"Wanna dance?"

"Okay."

I followed him out to a spot on the floor. He was okay-looking, but he never even said one word to me. When the song ended, he just walked off.

*Next.* But I didn't say it out loud.

Then I danced with two other guys—one named Brian and another guy who said his name was Franklin. Maybe he was giving me a fake name, or his last name.

But the next guy was Ethan, and he was definitely

the nicest of the four so far. He was cute. He had long blond skater hair that covered his eyes, and he was wearing jeans and skateboarding shoes. He kept tilting his head back to see out from under his hair.

After about three dances, it looked like Ethan wasn't interested in dancing with anyone else, which was fine with me.

When I saw Reb at the refreshment table, I asked Ethan if he wanted to get a drink. Reb was with a really cute guy named Cole.

"You two know each other?" Reb asked Cole and Ethan. They mumbled at each other. Guys have this weird nonverbal way of communicating.

"Well, you guys wait here. Kelly and I need to talk." Reb led me away.

"So how's it going? Do you like him?"

"Yeah, he's really nice. What about Cole? He's *cute*."

"Yeah, but he's got an ego the size of Montana. Look at Jennifer."

Jennifer was on the dance floor, still dancing with the same guy who'd first asked her. "Looks like she found her guy," Reb said with a smile. "Hey, take a look." She pointed to the dance floor. "Even Melissa found some poor loser to dance with her. He's definitely not her type."

Melissa's "loser" was kind of cute. He had dark curly

hair and a friendly face. If he'd asked me to dance, I would have. Melissa had pulled her hair back in a clip, and she had on a yellow cami and capri jeans. She looked sort of pretty.

"What's her type?" I wondered which of these guys Reb would consider my type.

"Social outcast." Reb looked around. "Now there. That guy standing over there. He looks like he'd be perfect for Melissa." She meant this skinny guy with a bad haircut and a lot of acne. "Want to do a little matchmaking?"

I looked over at Ethan. He looked bored. I didn't want to give him too many chances to find somebody else to dance with. "Maybe later. The guys are waiting for us."

When I got back to Ethan, he suggested we go out on the porch. It was dark now, but the porch lights were on. A lot of people were outside sitting on the porch's wood rails. Rachel was talking with a group of Crockett and Pine Haven counselors at the end of the porch, and when she saw me, she gave me a little wave. I didn't mind being seen with Ethan. It was definitely better than standing around with a bunch of girls, like some people were doing. And Ethan was getting cuter as the night went on.

Ethan had lots of funny stories about the guys in his cabin. I told him about short-sheeting Melissa, and he said he didn't know girls did stuff like that to each other. Then some counselors came by and made us all go back in.

When we walked in, Reb came charging over. "Hey, I've been looking all over for you! Look, Melissa and that guy aren't dancing anymore. Now's our chance to do some matchmaking."

"What happened to Cole? Where's Jennifer?" I just wanted to dance with Ethan right now. I wasn't sure what kind of matchmaking Reb was planning.

"I ditched him. And Jennifer's still attached to that same guy. So much for triplets. You and me are the Evil Twins on this one. Let's find Melissa the perfect match."

"Is that the girl you were talking about?" asked Ethan.

"Yeah." I looked at Reb. "I told him about short-sheeting Melissa. He thought it was funny."

"What are you going to do to her?"

"We're going to fix her up with somebody more her type," Reb explained. "Maybe that charming young man." She pointed out the guy we'd laughed at earlier.

"Oh, no, I got it! This'll be perfect!" Ethan's face lit up. "It's got to be Dustin Nesmith. He's in *my* cabin, and nobody can stand him. He's taken one shower this whole week, and that was because the counselor made him. Look, I'll tell him I know somebody who wants to dance with him. You tell her the same thing." Then he took off.

Reb grinned at me. "Ethan's cool. Okay, go over to Melissa and set it up. And don't act like it's any big deal for you to be talking to her."

Okay. This was weird. I'd barely talked to Melissa in days, and now I was supposed to go over and start a conversation? But I had to do it. I was a twin, wasn't I?

I walked up to Melissa with a little smile. "Hi. Having a good time?"

"I guess so." She was obviously surprised that I was suddenly talking to her again.

"Yeah, me too. I've been dancing with this guy, Ethan, and he has this friend who wants to dance with you. But he's kind of shy. He hasn't danced much, and"—she was giving me this weird look, like I had bean sprouts growing out of my ears—"anyway, he's over there. See those two guys? The one in the green shirt is Ethan, and that's his friend, Dustin."

Ethan and Dustin were across the floor, looking at us and talking. Dustin had a smirk on his face that didn't make him look at all shy. Melissa folded her arms across her chest like she had motion sickness or something.

"He looks like a nerd," she said.

"No, he doesn't." Although he did. "Do you have any idea how hard it is for a guy to ask a girl to dance? C'mon, just one dance."

"Well . . ."

Dustin was walking toward us, still with that awful smirk on his face. "Here he comes. Just don't break his heart."

CHAPTER 12

I kind of pushed Melissa toward Dustin and then met Ethan on the dance floor. I was looking around for Reb and finally saw her dancing with some new guy.

"So now what?" I asked Ethan.

Ethan shrugged. "Let's just wait and see what happens. When she gets a whiff of his body odor, she'll probably throw up on him."

Melissa and Dustin danced the next few dances, and we kept an eye on them the whole time. It seemed like Reb was watching them too, but somehow she and her latest guy had ended up halfway across the room. Dustin was talking between dances, but Melissa wasn't saying much.

When the next song started, the lights dimmed. It

was the first slow dance of the night. Ethan and I sort of grabbed each other in this weird way and started slow dancing. Watching Dustin and Melissa slow dance made me wonder if *we* looked that stupid. Dustin's knees were swaying back and forth like he was skiing down a mountain. Melissa had her hands behind his back, but it looked like she was trying not to touch him.

When that song ended, another slow song started. We just kept watching the two of them, which was good. It kept us from having to look at each other. It was the first time I'd ever slow danced with a boy. I was so glad I hadn't eaten any garlic bread.

Then something happened. Dustin and Melissa were slow dancing, and he had his hands on her back. But while I was watching them, I noticed that slowly, ever so slowly, he was moving his hands farther and farther down. Just how far was he planning to go? And didn't Melissa notice?

Then all of a sudden, when his hands went too far down, she jumped back out of his arms. Everyone around them looked at them. Melissa crossed her arms and walked away. She just left Dustin standing there.

Ethan was laughing so hard that now everyone was staring at *us*. "Did you see where his hands were?" he asked.

"YES! I can't believe she didn't slap him," I said.

"I wonder if any of the other guys saw it," he said, trying to make himself stop laughing. His eyes were watering and he needed a Kleenex.

I felt bad for Melissa. I wondered if Reb saw it. I looked around, but I couldn't see her in the crowd. Dustin had wandered off to stand with some other guys. He looked like he didn't care.

Then I had a thought—had Ethan put him up to it? Maybe he bribed him or dared him to do it. He sure thought it was funny. But would he do something that mean? Or was Dustin a complete freak on his own without any help from his friends?

Pretty soon they announced that it was the last song, and then the lights went back up and we all left the dining hall to go wait by the vans and trucks. Ethan walked out with me. "That was a lot of fun. I guess I'll see you at the next dance, huh?" he asked.

Wow, that was practically like asking for a second date! "Yeah! I had a good time tonight." Because I did. And I wanted him to know it.

"Yeah, me too. I'll see ya, Kelly." He kind of squeezed my hand before he walked away to where a bunch of guys were standing.

So. A hand squeeze. For a split second when we were

saying good-bye, I had a thought. What if he tried to kiss me? Wasn't that what you did at moments like this?

But he didn't. He didn't even come close. We'd been standing about two feet apart, and that's a huge space. How do you ever even close up a space that big?

I looked around at the big crowd of people wandering around. It was dark, but you could still see from the lights of the dining hall porch. I let out a sigh. My face felt hot. I was relieved. But also a little disappointed. It's weird that I could be both at the exact same time.

I finally saw Reb waiting by the white van we'd ridden over in. She grabbed my arm and dragged me around to the other side of the van. "Did you see it? Did you see what happened?" she asked me.

"Oh, you mean Dustin and Melissa?"

"Of course! What else? Did you see how he grabbed her! Why didn't we have a camera to capture the moment?" She held out her closed fist for me to pound it. "Excellent job setting her up. I can't believe how great it worked out!"

"Thanks." I'd been a good twin. But what if Ethan had done that to me when we were slow dancing? I probably would've reacted the same way Melissa did.

Then Rachel found us and made us get into the van. Jennifer had finally shown up. "That was the best dance

I've ever been to." She sighed. She looked lovesick and stupid.

"Ah, but you missed the highlight of the evening." Reb started whispering to her so I knew she was filling her in. Rachel had turned the van around, and the wheels crunched on the gravel road. "Did everyone have a good time?" she asked.

"I had a great time," Reb yelled. "Melissa, how 'bout you? Did you have a great time? I saw you dancing a lot." She'd turned around to Melissa, who was sitting on the bench behind us.

Melissa didn't answer. I couldn't tell what she was doing, since I didn't dare turn around. Did she think it was my fault Dustin did that to her? I certainly didn't put him up to it. Maybe I should try to talk to her tomorrow.

Reb rested her chin on the back of our seat. "Mewissa. Did oo hear me? Did oo have a gweat time?" she said in this annoying baby voice.

"Yeah." That was it. That's all she said. Why did Reb hate her so much? Sure, she was geeky, but I've seen geekier. There had to be a reason. What if, when camp started, I'd fallen into the "pick on" group instead of the "be nice to" group? What if Reb had really gotten mad that day I made the comment about her father, and she'd turned on me? It just seemed so random. What a relief to be Reb's friend, instead of her enemy.

"Hey, look," said Molly. "Jockey shorts. Lots of them." We looked out the windows, and hanging over the Camp Crockett sign, this wooden arch you drive under, were all these pairs of boys' underwear. And they were pink. And there was a huge sign made out of pink construction paper that said something we couldn't quite read.

"What did it say?" asked Jordan.

"Something about 'Thanks for a great dance from the . . .' and then I couldn't read the rest," said Erin.

"I think it said 'from the Pink Team,'" said Rachel. "What's up with that, Tis?"

Tisdale shook her head like she didn't have a clue. "Tsk, tsk. I guess some Pine Haven girls were up to some mischief."

## Tuesday, June 24

When we walked into the cabin from afternoon activities, we saw this huge canvas bag sitting by the door. On Sunday we'd sent all our dirty clothes out in a bag just like this one. "Yay! The laundry's here!" said Jennifer.

We had the cabin to ourselves, so the three of us dragged the bag to Side A.

"Let's dump it all out on Rachel's bed so we can find our stuff," said Reb. She immediately started smoothing out all her clothes and carefully folding them in a stack. I've never met anyone so neat in my life.

"Hey, that's my shirt," I said.

"Jennifer, this must be your bra." Reb swung it around her head like a lasso.

"Gimme that! You freak!"

"Whose bra is *this*?" I picked up a Little Mermaid training bra covered in pictures of Ariel. When Reb and Jennifer saw it, they both burst out laughing.

"Read the name tag to see whose it is," suggested Reb.

I wasn't crazy about examining someone else's bra up close, but I looked at the tag sewn inside. "Melissa's! Isn't that so sweet?" We all cracked up.

Reb gasped and pulled something out of the laundry pile. "Here are the undies that go with it!" The three of us were practically rolling on the floor, we were laughing so hard. I felt a little bad that we were making so much fun of them because it was pretty private. I mean, I wouldn't want someone looking at my underwear and laughing. But it was just so goofy. If my mom had packed something like that for me to bring to camp, I would've burned it the first day.

"Hey, hey, HEY!" Reb yelled. She had this maniac look in her eyes. "I've got a fabulous idea! Let's fly these from the flagpole so everybody in camp can appreciate them."

My stomach had the same nervous feeling I got when a teacher was passing out a test. "I don't know, Reb. Haven't we done enough? We short-sheeted her, and then that guy at the dance . . ."

"Kelly, c'mon. Remember the pink underwear? This is our chance to do something just as funny." There was a big debate about who'd pulled off the pink underwear prank at Camp Crockett Saturday night. Some people thought it was the CAs and others said it was the CATs. Neither group would admit to it.

"We'll get caught," I said. "Everybody'll see us."

"Not now, genius. Tonight. After everybody's asleep. We'll sneak out of the cabin and do it. Then tomorrow morning, they'll be flapping in the breeze."

"It'll be great!" Jennifer agreed. "The Terrible Triplets strike again." She fingered her wristband, which she was still wearing and had insisted that Reb and I keep on too. Reb thought it was stupid. I didn't mind it. I thought it was cool we all wore the same wristband.

"Exactly," Reb said. "We haven't been very terrible lately. We'll lose our reputation. Okay, here's what we'll do. . . ."

Once Reb made up her mind about something, there was no stopping her. She really was amazing. As I listened to her, I could tell she was working out all the details in her head as she went along. And she had thought of everything.

She said we should wait till two a.m. to make sure all the counselors were back from kitchen raids. She said she'd try to stay awake, but just in case, she had a little alarm clock she would put under her pillow so no one else would hear it. She kept stressing how quiet we had to be so we wouldn't get caught.

"What about flashlights?" Jennifer asked.

"Too risky. Somebody might see the light. It's not that far to the flagpole."

So that was the plan. I felt jittery, but in a good way. It would be a challenge to sneak out of the cabin and pull off this prank without getting caught. And then the whole camp would wake up and find a Little Mermaid bra and panties flying from the flagpole. It *was* pretty funny. And anyway, nobody would know whose underwear it was. Except us. And Melissa, of course. It wasn't *that* embarrassing.

Later everyone came in and picked out their clothes. If Melissa noticed that some of her underwear was missing, she didn't say anything. We could hardly wait for night to come.

Rachel should've suspected something, because we all got in bed with no fuss. Then we just lay there in the dark, waiting. I kept shifting from my side to my back to my stomach. Lights out was ten o'clock. That meant we had a four-hour wait.

"Quit flopping around over there," Reb whispered. "I'm trying to sleep."

"Sorry." I smiled. *Good cover, Reb*. I closed my eyes and tried to be still.

And then, about fifteen minutes later, Reb was shaking me. She put her hand over my mouth and whispered, "It's time."

Good thing she'd covered up my mouth, because I kind of grunted. Two a.m.? Already? Then I noticed how quiet and still everything was. I sat up on the edge of my bed, and my head was heavy.

I'd stuffed a pair of jeans and a dark blue T-shirt under my covers, so I pulled those out and slipped them on. Jennifer climbed down from the top bunk like a burglar.

A shadow stood by the bunk beds, and even though I knew it was Reb, it still sort of freaked me out because it was so dark and I couldn't see her face at all. The shadow motioned toward the door, and Jennifer and I tiptoed behind. I could just make out the outlines of Melissa and Rachel sleeping in their cots a few feet away. I held my breath as I crept past them.

We all three stopped at the door. Slowly Reb put out her hand and pushed gently against the screen door. It opened with a soft groan. All three of us froze and waited. Nobody stirred, so Reb waved at us to go through. We slipped soundlessly through the door.

# CHAPTER 14

Whew. We'd made it outside. I let all my air out like a balloon deflating. We walked down Middler Line, the only sound our sneakers padding along the soft dirt path. It felt strange to be out in the middle of the night. The air was cool and everything was perfectly quiet, but it wasn't the same as it was during the day when everyone was at activities and the cabins were empty. You could kind of *feel* everyone asleep in the cabins. I looked up, and the sky was velvet black with a million little sparks of silver. Reb was right. There was enough light for us to see.

But when we got to the steps going down to the lodge, it was pitch-black from all the trees. Now we could barely see. We were stumbling down the stone steps when I felt a hand brush past my arm. Then there was this huge thud and a scream. I could just make out a dark form at the bottom of the steps. It was Jennifer, lying there in a heap.

"What happened?" Reb whispered at her hoarsely. Jennifer groaned in pain.

"Uh, I . . . slipped." I could hear her suck in her breath.

"Are you hurt?" Reb's voice sounded worried.

"Um, yeah . . . my ankle. I twisted it."

"Oh great! It could be sprained. We gotta get you to the cabin . . . or the infirmary. Kelly, give me a hand." She swung one of Jennifer's arms over her shoulder, and I took the other.

"Oh, stop it! It's not *that* bad. I can make it to the flagpole, at least." She pulled away from us and took a few careful steps.

"Look, I do a lot of sports, and you shouldn't mess around with injuries. You could hurt it even more by walking on it. We've got to go back."

"No way are we going back now! How can you even suggest that?" Jennifer's voice rose, and Reb and I both shushed her.

"Don't you think your ankle is more important than some stupid prank?"

I couldn't help smiling. It was sweet that she was so worried about Jennifer. She really was loyal to her friends.

"Listen. It's my ankle. I know how it feels. And I'm telling you—it's fine. I know for sure I can make it. Let's just go." Jennifer limped ahead of us. Reb reached out and grabbed her by the elbow for added support. We really didn't have very far to go. The flagpole was just past the lodge near the top of the hill.

When we got there, we all looked up to the top of it at the same time. Reb reached inside her jacket and pulled out Melissa's bra and underwear. "Give me a hand."

For some reason Jennifer and I both applauded softly, and then we laughed because we'd thought of the same thing.

"No kidding." Reb sounded annoyed. "I've never done this before."

I helped her untie the rope looped around the pole. It made my hands cold to touch the bare steel. The metal clasps on the rope banged against the pole and made a hollow clang. Next we hooked the bra through the top clasp and put the bottom clasp through one of the panty legs. Then we pulled the rope to raise the underwear up and tied the rope in place.

"Mission accomplished," Reb said, and we all slapped hands. We looked up at the underwear at the top of the pole. We could barely see it. One thing was for sure—Melissa's underwear wasn't nearly as big as a flag.

"It might be funnier if Melissa was, like, a D-cup," said Jennifer.

"Maybe we should salute and then sing 'Under the Sea.' Wait—make that 'Under the Shirt.'" Reb snapped to attention like an army guy and was about to start singing when I clapped my hand over her mouth. We all laughed.

All of a sudden Jennifer grabbed my arm. I looked at her, but she was staring at something off in the distance. "I just saw something move!"

"Where?" Reb and I both whispered. All the blood drained down my legs and I was frozen in icy terror.

"There! In front of Crafts Cabin."

"I don't see anything," Reb whispered back.

"But I did! And it was somebody. But they're out of sight now," Jennifer insisted.

"Well, let's just go," Reb suggested.

"No! They'll see us!" Jennifer hissed. She was still staring at the same spot.

"Then we should definitely get out of here!" For the first time ever, Reb actually sounded scared, and that made me feel like having a full-blown panic attack. There was somebody else out here, creeping around in the dark, maybe *watching* us?

We started moving. Should we run or walk or creep? We mostly crept. When we got to the steps by the lodge, we figured we were out of sight from any "night stalkers."

"Jennifer, how ya doing? Are you gonna make it?"

"Yeah, it's okay. It hurts a little, but I can walk on it."

"She may be okay, but I'm dying," I groaned in agony.

"What's wrong with *you*?"

"I've *got* to go to Solitary. Jennifer made me so nervous I can't hold it anymore."

"*Now*? You have to go *now*?"

"No, tomorrow morning will be just fine," I snapped back at her.

"What next?" Reb growled. "Well, c'mon. We'll be going right by there, anyway."

We stopped at the top of the steps. "You go ahead. We'll wait here."

I took short, quick steps so I wouldn't lose my grip. The lights of Solitary practically blinded me after being in the dark, and I staggered into my favorite stall—the third one on the left, which had a little poem on the wall inside: *If you sprinkle when you tinkle, please be neat and wipe the seat.*

I sat there and read that poem for the 437th time. I sighed, feeling so much better. But when I flushed, the toilet was so loud I was afraid I'd wake the whole camp. I stood still, waiting for the noise to stop. Then I stepped out of the door of Solitary and walked down the line to where Reb and Jennifer were waiting.

"Hold it!"

Every muscle in my body froze. My heart stopped and my knees buckled. All the air went out of my lungs and I stood still, paralyzed.

"Where do you think *you're* going?"

# CHAPTER 15

I think I stood frozen in that one spot for about ten minutes, maybe more. Not breathing. Not moving. A muscle in my face twitched, and I locked my knees to keep them from folding up. Slowly, ever so slowly, I looked around.

Behind me was Libby Sheppard, one of the swimming counselors. We both stood there in this little patch of light shining from Solitary, looking at each other. Good thing I'd already gone to the bathroom. I was shaking so hard now I couldn't hold my legs still.

Libby had on a sundress, and her purse was over her arm. She must've just gotten back from leave. Leave! All that careful planning—we'd never even thought of that.

"Where ya going?" Libby asked me again.

"I don't feel very good," I said, my voice quavering. No lie there. My heart was hammering so hard it felt like it was going to pop out of my chest any minute now, like an alien. If she needed more proof, I was sure I could puke my guts out right now with very little effort.

Libby frowned at me. "You don't look very good. Are you sick?"

"Yeah!" I said it a little too loudly. But maybe loud was a good thing. Maybe Reb and Jennifer would hear me and stay out of sight. Had Libby seen the underwear? Was she the one we'd seen lurking around?

If I could keep Libby's eyes on me and away from where Reb and Jennifer were hiding, maybe things wouldn't get any worse than they already were.

"Who's your counselor . . . Rachel?"

"Ah, yeah. But I didn't want to wake her up."

"Oh." Libby looked at me closely. Was she concerned or suspicious? I really couldn't tell. "Want me to walk you to the infirmary?"

"No. I mean, I feel better now. I think I'll just try to get some sleep." I put one foot behind me, ready to turn around and walk off, if Libby would just let me go.

"Hold on a second. You should probably go. There's

some kind of virus going around, you know. A bunch of girls have ended up in the infirmary. C'mon. I'll walk you down there."

Oh, great! Now would she force me to go to the infirmary? I needed a way out. I stuck my hands in my jeans pockets and looked up at Libby, trying to put a pitiful expression on my face. "Well, I'll tell you something, if you promise not to say anything to anybody, okay?"

Libby nodded, all reassuring and everything.

"Well . . . this is kind of embarrassing. I was homesick. Tonight, all of a sudden, I started missing my parents, especially my mom. All because of dinner."

"What about dinner?" Libby asked.

"Well, it was awful. Stewed tomatoes make me gag, literally. And then I'm not crazy about black-eyed peas, either."

Libby laughed.

"Anyway, I was thinking about my mom's cooking and wondering what *my* family was having for supper. And that just made me think about everything at home. I felt lonely, so I was going to the infirmary to talk to the nurse. But after I got dressed, I wasn't crazy about walking down there in the dark."

We walked over and sat down on the steps to Solitary.

"So you're sure you're not sick?" Libby put her hand on my forehead, and that actually made my chest tighten a little bit, because my mom does the exact same thing.

"No. I guess I just needed someone to talk to." I smiled at her. Might as well lay it on thick.

"You know, I was homesick my first summer at Pine Haven too."

"Really?" I asked. Wow. We were actually having a moment.

"Yeah." Libby laughed, remembering. "It was terrible. I was ten, and I hated, I mean absolutely *despised* camp. I wrote my parents all the time, begging them to come get me. But then I started having a great time, and I cried when my parents came to pick me up, 'cause I didn't want to leave."

I smiled. "I won't tell about you being homesick if you won't tell about me. Deal?"

"Deal! Well, are you gonna be okay now?"

"Yeah." I stood up and breathed. I'd managed to get out of this, amazingly. "Thanks a lot, Libby. I feel a whole lot better now."

"Sure." She gave me a quick hug, and then I headed toward Cabin 1 and she went toward Cabin 3. I prayed that Reb and Jennifer would figure it out and come back to the cabin when the coast was clear.

I tried to be as quiet as we'd been earlier, but all I really wanted to do was get in bed as fast as I could. I could see one big lump in Rachel's bed and a smaller lump in Melissa's bed, but both Reb's and Jennifer's bunks were still empty.

I got into bed and pulled off my jeans. I lay there and tried to hold my trembling legs still. Where were those guys? What if Libby caught them, too? Did Libby believe me? If she'd seen us at the flagpole, why didn't she bust me right then?

For two eternities I lay there waiting. I was about to go stark raving mad when I heard the screen door open very softly. My heart leaped in relief. Two shadows came in. They didn't make a sound. I knew it was Reb and Jennifer, but they were so quiet and so dark, it was a little scary to watch them.

I was dying to whisper to them, to find out if everything was okay. But I didn't dare. I just lay there. Reb slipped into her bed, and Jennifer climbed up to the top bunk with the springs squeaking a couple of times. It didn't matter, though, because the beds always squeak when someone turns over.

I could almost *feel* Reb and Jennifer wanting to say something to me. But not now. Too much had happened. We couldn't chance it. Talking could wait till morning. It would *have* to.

# CHAPTER 16

## Wednesday, June 25

The next morning, when the rising bell rang at eight o'clock, it took every ounce of energy I had to drag myself out of bed. My brain felt like it was covered with a layer of fuzz. How many hours of sleep did we get, anyway? Three? Four, maybe?

With everyone around, we still couldn't talk about our adventure, but we gave each other quick, silent looks. All I could think about was how pretty soon everyone would see a Little Mermaid bra and panties up the flagpole.

We had to do our morning chores before inspection. After I'd finished sweeping and Jennifer and Reb had made their beds and emptied the trash, the three of us took off together for the dining hall.

Thankfully, Jennifer had only a slight limp this morning.

"I'm glad you're okay," said Reb. "It'd be tough to explain how you sprained your ankle in the middle of the night. You really had me scared you'd hurt it bad."

"It's fine. I told you that last night," Jennifer replied. It was cool that Reb was so concerned about her. I knew that if anything ever happened to me, she had my back.

As we passed the lodge, we could see the flagpole. And there was Melissa's underwear, in broad daylight now. The panties were just hanging there limp, but the bra was caught in a little breeze.

"Ah, look at our hard work." Reb sighed.

The funny thing was, Chris Ramirez and Maggie Windsor walked right under the flagpole and didn't once look up. I guess some people wouldn't notice if their hair was on fire. I was beginning to wonder if maybe nobody would notice, or if people did, then maybe they wouldn't even think it was funny.

But then a group of girls walked by, and one of them, JD Duckworth, saw the underwear and started laughing. "Attention! Is anyone missing some lingerie?" She stood there and made sure that everyone walking by saw them. JD was a complete nutcase. She actually got caught by the Porch Patrol at the dance last week.

"It's so perfect that JD's the one who saw them!" whispered Jennifer.

"I know!" Reb agreed. We stopped under the flagpole with everyone else, acting totally innocent.

Reb cupped her hands over her eyes and looked up. "Why, JD—is that underwear I see?"

JD looked up too. "Why, yes, Rebecca, I believe it is. Are you missing any undergarments?"

Reb patted her chest like she was checking. "Nope. Not me. All my underwear is present and accounted for."

"Well, it's not mine, either. I think the bra belongs to somebody who's an A cup. Hey, Jessica—what's your bra size?" she yelled at this girl walking by.

As we stood there, we saw that Melissa was walking this way with a totally oblivious look on her face. Now JD was yelling at the top of her lungs, "Attention! Attention! Would the owner of an Ariel bra and panty set please report to the flagpole immediately?"

The three of us watched Melissa's every move. It was like you could read her mind. First she saw all of us standing around. Then, since we were looking up, she looked up too. Her forehead crinkled and her eyes squinted, like she was thinking, *Is that what I think it is?* Then she looked down really quick, like she didn't want to make eye contact anymore.

"Well, hi, Melissa," said Reb, all friendly. "Do you know anyone who's missing Little Mermaid underwear?" Nobody thought anything about the question, since JD had been harassing every single girl who walked by, asking her bra size. But Melissa actually jumped when Reb said that to her. She didn't make a sound, though. She looked at Reb, then she looked away, and then she took off for the dining hall without looking back.

"She must really be hankering for a bowl of Wheaties!" Reb had her elbow propped on my shoulder, and then she bent over and laughed so hard I thought everyone would suspect what was going on, but nobody did.

Inside the dining hall nobody at our table said anything about the underwear, but halfway through breakfast, Cabin 2's table clapped their hands to signal that they had a "parley-voo" to sing. Parley-voos were songs that campers made up to sing about some sort of camp news—like missing underwear.

> *Somebody lost her bra today, parley-voo.*
> *Somebody lost her bra today, parley-voo.*
> *Somebody lost her bra today.*
> *She's too flat to need it, anyway!*
> *Inky, dinky, parley-voo!*

JD was in Cabin 2, so I was sure she was the master-mind behind that one.

After breakfast somebody had taken the underwear down, but at least everyone in camp had already seen them.

"We've got to go someplace private to talk," Reb whispered to us. She was right. The three of us hadn't been alone since last night.

We decided to get our tennis rackets and go to the tennis courts. Tis and the other counselors weren't there yet, so we sat down at the end of the court with our backs against the fence. Finally we had some privacy.

"Triplets rule!" said Jennifer. She made us all touch wristbands, which Reb always thought was pretty stupid, but I thought it was fun.

"I can't believe we actually pulled it off!" I said.

"Yeah, but who took them down?" broke in Jennifer. "All that work getting them up there and then—"

"Hey, it doesn't matter, though," Reb interrupted. "If anything, it makes it more mysterious. Like, first they're up there, then they're gone."

"But Kelly, what happened when Libby caught you? We almost died when we heard her!" Jennifer gasped.

"*You* almost died! I almost wet my pants! But then I opened my mouth, and this whole involved story came out about how I was homesick and wanted someone to talk to, and blah, blah, blah. I never knew I could lie like that!"

"You did an amazing job of thinking on your feet," said Reb.

"Yeah," I agreed, loving the compliment, but I was worried about something. "But what if Libby suspects that I put the underwear up there? She did catch me wandering around in the middle of the night."

"So what?" asked Reb.

"She could tell Eda."

"Yeah, you're right." Reb sounded worried. "Then Eda would make you fly your own undies from the flagpole every day for the rest of camp, and we'd all have to stand there and salute while you raised them."

"Oh, shut up!" I gave her a shove.

Reb laughed. "The best part, though, the *best*, was Melissa's face when she saw her bra and panties flying from the flagpole! That was un-freaking-believable! I wish I'd had a camera!"

By now people were showing up, so we had to quit talking. We asked Santana Hickman to play with us in doubles. She and Reb destroyed Jennifer and me, but Reb showed me a couple of things about my serve, and it actually got a lot better.

When we walked past the flagpole after morning activities, we noticed that the flag was in place. "Do you think Melissa will get her underwear back?" I asked.

"Jeez! Who cares? It's just underwear! You act like you've never had a practical joke played on you."

"Have *you*?" I asked, because I couldn't imagine Reb ever being a victim.

"Are you kidding? *All* the time. I live with the two biggest practical jokers on the planet—my dad and Zach."

Jennifer raised her eyebrows. "Really? Like what do they do?"

Reb rolled her eyes. "Oh anything and everything. Too many to count." She paused for a second. "Like this one time—the first time we ever went skiing. I was just a tiny kid, about five I think, and I was terrified of riding the lifts. So Dad said he'd ride with me, and when we were way up high, he rocked our chair back and forth, and he looked all panicked, and he goes, 'Uh-oh, I think there's an avalanche coming!' When we got to the top of the lift, Dad practically had to peel my fingernails out of the back of the chair. He laughed his butt off over that one. And Zach, he'd pinned a note to the back of my jacket that said, 'Throw snowballs at me,' and I couldn't figure out why this group of boys kept laughing and pelting me with snowballs."

Jennifer had slowed down so she was walking slightly behind Reb. She gave me this look—her forehead wrinkled, her mouth hanging open. I looked back at her and raised one eyebrow, like, *I know! I can't believe it either!* But we both knew to keep our mouths shut.

"A few practical jokes never hurt anyone," Reb went on. "They toughen you up, keep you on your guard. I mean, just look at Melissa. Don't you think she could use a little toughening up?"

Jennifer and I were quiet, and Reb looked at us both. "Well?"

"Absolutely," said Jennifer.

I was glad Jennifer had said something, because I didn't want to answer that question. The morning had started off so exciting—I could hardly wait to see the Little Mermaid underwear in daylight. But now I had a sad feeling in my stomach. I couldn't stop picturing a little five-year-old Reb being pelted with snowballs and tormented on a ski lift by her own father. And I was still kind of worried about whether Melissa would ever get her undies back.

So Reb and Melissa actually had something in common—they'd both been picked on. But Reb had been picked on by her own family. How weird was that? Which was worse? To have your family tease you, or other kids—like at school or camp? So far nobody had ever really picked on me, except one time in second grade this boy, Jacob Townsend, kept sticking his pencil in my hair. Ms. McCord moved him to another desk, and then he didn't bother me again.

But you just never knew when the crowd might turn on you for no reason. Anyone could be the victim. It was so hard to predict.

# CHAPTER 17

## Friday, June 27

"Well, that was exhausting." I peeled off my grimy jeans and collapsed on my bunk. We'd just gotten back from a three-mile hike to Lookout Point.

Reb was sprawled across her cot too. Jennifer stood in front of the mirror and clenched her teeth. I wondered what kind of face she made before she got braces.

"A swim in the lake would be great right now," Reb suggested. "Can't you just feel that cold water?" Her blond hair was all sweaty and stuck against her neck.

"Yeah," I moaned. "Why don't you carry me down there and throw me in?"

Just then Melissa walked in. She kind of glanced at us like she wanted to walk right out the door again, but she didn't.

"Hi," I said, because I never wanted to completely ostracize her.

"Hi," she answered, but she didn't really look at me.

Reb sat up and waved at her like she was her BFF. "Hey there, MA-LISS-AH! So, how've ya been? Liking camp so far? Whaddaya think of the food? Been getting lots of e-mails from Mom and Dad? World been treatin' ya . . . okay?" Reb was talking really fast, like an auctioneer.

"I guess so," Melissa said, glancing at Reb and then looking away.

"Really? That's SUPER! I'm *glad* to hear it!" Reb shouted.

Melissa turned her back to us and put on her robe, then slung a towel over her shoulder. She edged out the door like she was afraid Reb was going to pounce on her.

"See ya!" Reb yelled, all cheerful, and gave her another big wave. Then she looked at us, all sad. "Gee whiz. She's not very friendly."

"Maybe we should just leave her alone." I meant it to sound like, *Yeah, you're right, she's not friendly, so let's just leave her alone*, but it didn't come out right. There was this huge silence. Jennifer looked at Reb, then me, then back at Reb.

"What do you mean by that?" Reb asked. She locked her eyes on me, and it made me nervous.

"Nothing. Just—you know, she obviously wants to avoid us, so . . ."

Reb sat there with this really straight look on her face. She didn't look mad or threatening, but she kept looking at me like she was waiting for me to say something else.

"Are we going swimming?" I asked. I got up to get my suit from my trunk.

"I don't know, Kelly. Is that what you want to do?" Reb asked.

"Yeah, I guess. If you guys want to." I tried not to look at her.

"Okay, then. Let's go." We all changed clothes, but everyone was pretty quiet. As we were leaving, Jennifer said, "This will feel good. I hope the water's freezing." She glanced at me, then at Reb, trying to read the signs.

"Yeah, me too," I said. Reb stared straight ahead. The only thing worse than her staring at me was the silent treatment.

We were walking past Solitary and the showers when Reb stopped us all of a sudden. "Do you see what I see? Over the door of Shower Number Two?" She pointed.

There were six showers in a row, each with a green wooden door and a big white number painted on it. Hanging over the door of Shower 2, we could see

Melissa's white robe and baby blue towel—the same ones she'd walked out with five minutes ago.

Reb put her arms around both of our necks, like we were in a football huddle. She was kind of smiling. "This is soooooo tempting. So, so tempting." She looked at Jennifer, then at me. "What do you say, triplets? Should we? Or shouldn't we?"

Usually Jennifer would be all over it, but this time she kept quiet and looked at me. Now, all of a sudden, Reb was her old self, and she was talking to me again.

"This is too good to pass up," I said. There was nothing else I could say.

Reb's grin was a mile wide. "Okay, who wants to do it?"

I looked at the door and then back at Reb. "I will. I'm a pretty fast runner." We were still huddled together, and Reb grabbed my shoulder, like she was pepping me up for the big play. "Okay. Try not to make too much noise. If you're fast enough, she might not even see them go."

I headed straight for the showers. My heart was beating faster. I could hear the water running inside the stall. The towel and robe were right in front of me. All I had to do was reach out and grab them. I held my hand up. I could feel Jennifer and Reb behind me, watching. With one quick move, I grabbed the towel and robe and pulled them over the top of the door. I clutched them against my chest and took off running. Did someone yell inside the shower? I wasn't sure. I was halfway down the line now, running as fast as I could. I crashed through the cabin door with Reb and Jennifer right behind me. My heart pounded in my chest, and I was gasping for breath.

I held up the towel and robe to show them. "Now what?" I panted.

Reb looked around. "Quick! Put it with the other ones!" She pointed to a stack of identical blue towels on the wooden shelf by Melissa's bed. In a rush, I folded it up and stuck it under the others at the bottom of the stack.

"What about the robe?" I yelled, holding it up and looking around.

"Just hang it up someplace!" Jennifer shouted.

I grabbed an empty wire hanger from the metal rod that was over the beds and hung the robe up with the other clothes. Then we ran out the door, crashing right into Jordan and Molly coming back from their riding lesson.

"What's with you?" Molly yelled at us, jumping out of our way.

"Nothing! Sorry!" Reb yelled as we ran down the line.

"Over here." Reb led us to some bushes between Cabin 4 and Solitary. We could see the showers from here, but we were kind of hidden from anyone walking by.

"Is she still in there?" Jennifer wondered.

"Of course she is," Reb said. "Nobody's seen a naked streak go by at a hundred miles an hour, have they?" We all laughed at the thought.

Jennifer gave us a sly look. "How *is* she going to get out of there?"

Reb shrugged. "She can just waltz right out the door anytime she wants. It's not like we *locked* her in there. Anyway, this *is* a girls' camp. Big deal if she's naked."

Jennifer snorted. "Reb, you know Miss Modest is never coming out of there without a towel on. She'll stay there till Closing Day if she has to."

"Jennifer's right. Maybe we should give them back now," I said. I have to admit—it had been a huge rush to steal them in the first place, but now . . . well, there was really no way for her to get out of the shower unless we gave them back.

"Oh, good idea," Reb said, "and then let's beg her forgiveness for short-sheeting her and flying her underwear up the flagpole."

"Well, how long should she stay in there?" I asked. I'd let her call all the shots.

"Shhh, someone's coming," Reb said. "It's Erin."

From our hideout, we could see Erin walking down the line, and as she passed the showers, she stopped and looked around. We could tell that the door to Shower 2 had opened a little, and Erin was talking to the person hidden inside. Then she looked around and walked away.

Jennifer stared at us. "She's leaving her in there?" she whispered.

"Don't count on it. She's probably getting her a towel," Reb said.

She was right. Five minutes later Erin was back, carrying a baby blue towel just like the one that had mysteriously disappeared. Then Melissa came out of the shower stall with the towel around her. Her wet hair was plastered against her head, and her ears stuck through it. She looked even more pathetic than usual. Well, at least she'd gotten out of there. She was really only stranded in there a couple of minutes.

Melissa and Erin were whispering together. "I don't know! I didn't see them!" I heard Melissa say. They went to the cabin.

Jennifer sighed. "Too bad. Fun's over."

"Not quite. It's probably just beginning. Let's go."

Back at the cabin, Reb burst through the door.

"Hey, cabinmates, what's new?" Melissa was rummaging through her open trunk, still wrapped in the towel. Molly and Jordan were on Side B, acting extremely interested in their card game.

Erin stood by the door and frowned at us. "Melissa was taking a shower, and somebody stole her robe and towel." She looked at us like, *Quit being such jerks.* Erin was way too mature to ever play any pranks like ours. I felt stupid in front of her.

"Really?" Reb gasped, all shocked. "Your things were stolen! That's terrible! Hope you had name tags in them. We'll keep an eye out for them." She had her hands behind her back, and she looked all concerned. "What'd they look like?"

Melissa slammed her trunk closed and gave Reb a killer look. "Well, it just so happens—I found both my towel and my robe when I got back." She waved to where we'd put her stuff away. She was trying to sound sarcastic, but her voice was all quavery.

"No kidding? Maybe you just forgot to take them with you, huh?"

"Oh, right! I just walked down to the showers naked! I know you guys did it. Don't deny it." She was madder than I'd ever seen her.

"Now what makes you so sure of that? We were at

the lake," Reb said. All three of us had on swimsuits.

"Oh, really? How come you're not wet?"

On the verge of hysterics, Melissa had still managed to point out this minor inconsistency in our story.

"Jennifer got her period, so we had to come back."

"*Reb!*" Jennifer slapped her on the arm, all embarrassed.

"Look, Melissa," Reb went on. "I'm just as upset as you are. I certainly don't want to see you naked." Then we walked out the door.

At least Melissa didn't cry. I was glad about that.

# CHAPTER 18

## Tuesday, July 1

"Hey, Jennifer, race you!" Reb and I were paddling around in one canoe, and Jennifer was by herself in another.

"You must be joking. I can't even get this stupid thing to go straight."

"How about if I paddle with you?" I offered. I looked over my shoulder at Reb in the stern. "Do you mind?"

"Fine with me." Reb made little circles in the water with her paddle.

"Let's go back to shore so I can get in with Jennifer."

"No way. That's on the other side of the lake. Just climb in. We're close enough."

We had paddled over to Jennifer, and she reached out to grab the gunwales of our canoe to pull us even closer.

I gave Jennifer my paddle and stood up slowly because moving around made the canoe rock a little. Carefully I put one foot in Jennifer's canoe and was about to bring the other leg across when she let go of the side. That made the canoes drift apart, and I lost my balance. I heard Reb yell, "Whoa!" just as I hit the water.

Green lake water swallowed me up for a couple of seconds before I could come up for air. The water was so cold it kind of shocked me, falling in like that.

"Are you okay?" Reb yelled. I'd come up between the two canoes, and I couldn't see either her or Jennifer.

"Yeah, fine," I answered. I snorted to get the water out of my nose and flipped the wet hair out of my eyes.

"Wow, that was worth seeing." Reb sounded like she was trying not to laugh.

"Just get me back in before I freeze to death, okay?"

Jennifer was trying to help me in. It wasn't easy because when I was climbing in, the canoe was tilting like crazy. Jennifer came real close to falling out on top of me.

When I finally got in and sat down, Reb and Jennifer both looked like they'd just wiped smiles off their faces. I tried to look mad, but then I started laughing, which made them both laugh too.

"I'll have to change now!" I complained. "Take me back to shore."

So we paddled back across the lake. Michelle Burns, the canoeing counselor, looked at us like we were a bunch of goofs. She was busy with serious canoers who went on river trips, and I could tell she was a little annoyed that we were playing around.

"Did you have a little trouble?" she asked us as I climbed out of the canoe.

"Yeah. Those two—they're a bad influence. I've got to change."

Reb dragged her canoe up on the bank and then waded out into the water to climb in with Jennifer. "Well, hurry. You can paddle solo when you get back."

"Aren't you coming with me?" I looked at them both.

"Hey, you're the one who needs to change, not us," said Jennifer, which made me mad. I never would've fallen in if I hadn't been trying to help her.

"Just hurry and come back," said Reb. "We'll be waiting for you."

I could tell they weren't going anywhere. I thought about just staying in my wet clothes, but it was cloudy and I was already starting to shiver.

As I walked away, I saw Libby Sheppard waving at me. She was across the lake, giving a swimming lesson. Ever since that night in Solitary, Libby had been really nice to me, smiling every time she saw me and always saying hi. I felt bad. She thought of me as a sweet little homesick camper who needed some extra attention. Little did she know I was a bold-faced liar.

I walked up the hill, my shoes squishing with every step. I was really shivering now. Thick clouds covered the sky, and it looked like it was going to rain.

When I got to the cabin, I was about to walk in when I heard something. I flattened myself against the wall and ducked down so I wouldn't be seen through the screen.

Inside, somebody was crying. Slowly I raised my head up. I pressed my forehead against the screen so I could look inside the dark cabin without being seen.

I already had a pretty good idea who it was, and I was right. I could just see the end of Melissa's bed, and she was lying there, facedown, crying into her pillow. I ducked down again to keep out of sight.

Great. I really needed to change. My clothes were absolutely sopping wet. I couldn't go back to the lake like this. But I didn't want to go in there now and face Melissa. What was wrong with her, anyway? Well, I had a pretty good idea. I stood there, trying to decide what to do. Then it sounded like the crying stopped. I was about to take off running because I was afraid she'd come out the door any second now, and she'd catch me. But then I heard her moving around inside. So very carefully, I stood up a little to peek inside again.

What I saw almost gave me a heart attack. Melissa was kneeling over Reb's trunk, digging through all her stuff! I couldn't believe it! I was catching her in the act of stealing something from Reb's trunk! But wait, that wasn't it. She was *searching* it.

She was going through all of Reb's stuff very carefully, and she looked like she was trying to put everything back where she'd found it. If she was looking for something to steal, she was being awfully selective.

Then she closed the lid. And next she moved on to Jennifer's trunk! Now I had no doubt. Melissa was definitely looking for *something*.

I couldn't believe it! I freaking couldn't believe what I was seeing. Should I go get Reb and Jennifer right now? Or just burst in and catch her in the act? Before I could make up my mind, Melissa made it up for me. Because when she'd finished with Jennifer's trunk, she moved over to mine! Now she'd really gone too far. I jumped right up and rushed for the door. I slammed the screen door open as I burst inside. Melissa was still sitting there in front of my open trunk when she turned around.

"You better shut that trunk before I slam it on your *face!*"

CHAPTER 19

Melissa was so shocked, she almost fell right into my open trunk. I was furious! It was bad enough that I'd seen her looking through my best friends' trunks, but here I'd caught her—red-handed—looking through mine.

"What do you think you're *doing*?"

Her mouth hung open and she was still frozen, squatting there in front of my trunk. "Ah. . . ." That was all she could manage to say.

"And not just *my* trunk. I was watching you! I saw you going through Reb's and Jennifer's trunks. Are you *stealing* from us?" I yelled. I stood there, dripping wet, my arms crossed in front of my chest. I felt like I had to hold myself in so I didn't punch her.

She drew back a little, staring at me. "Why are you so wet?"

"I fell in the freaking lake! What are you doing in my trunk?"

Melissa glanced down at the open lid. One of my shirts had fallen out and was lying on the wood floor. She knew she was busted. "I . . . I lost something," she finally mumbled.

"Lost something? Well, you didn't lose it in Reb's or Jennifer's trunks, and I can guarantee you didn't lose it in *mine*!"

Melissa frowned at me. "I know this looks terrible. But honestly, I was just looking for something of mine. I've looked everywhere for it. Maybe I lost it." Then she looked directly at me. "Or maybe it was stolen."

My mouth fell open. "Okay, let me get this straight. I catch you searching all our trunks, and now you're accusing us of stealing? We would never steal anything."

"Oh, no!" Melissa yelled all of a sudden. "No, *you* wouldn't do *that*." Even though she was mad, her voice was all quavery. "But you *would* short-sheet a person's bed, and you *would* take a person's towel when she's in the shower, and you *would* fly a person's underwear from the flagpole for the whole camp to see and laugh at! You *would* do all *those* things, but you would never *steal* anything!"

She was so obviously out of line, going through our trunks. But now . . . now I couldn't think of how to turn things back around to blaming her. We just stood there, glaring at each other. There was a little puddle around my shoes where I'd dripped. My arms and legs were all broken out in goose bumps, and I just wanted to put on some dry clothes. I wasn't looking for some major fight.

"What did you lose, anyway?" I finally asked her.

"My bracelet!"

And then she started to cry. Not a little sniffle, with tears welling up in her eyes. She was bawling. Out loud. "I lost my bracelet! My grandmother gave it to me! It was hers when she was young. And she died last year!" Man. She was sobbing!

"I never take it off. Except to swim or take a shower. And then I always put it in a safe place in my trunk. And now it's gone! It's lost forever!"

I just stood there, shocked by how upset she was. I should say something. Or do something. I just didn't know what. What I really wanted to do more than anything was just walk out the door. But she was crying so hard, I was kind of scared she might hyperventilate or rupture a blood vessel or something. She sat down on her bed, and now she was holding her head in her hands and was making that hiccuping sound you make when you've been crying for a really long time.

Finally, after standing there for what seemed like an hour, with her crying and me dripping, very quietly I went over to my trunk. It was still open. I got out some dry clothes and changed as fast as I could.

Now I could leave, but I knew I had to say something. "Look, Melissa. I'm sorry you lost your bracelet. Obviously it means a lot to you. But I swear—we didn't steal it."

"Oh, and I'm supposed to take your word for it?" She looked up at me. Her face was all blotchy, and her eyes were red and swollen, but also full of anger that almost looked like hatred. "Why do you go along with them on *everything*? Why are you so *mean* to me?"

I never tried to be mean. Reb was always coming up with these ideas, and . . . I just went along with them. Melissa never seemed that upset about it, until now.

I hung up my wet clothes so I'd have something to do, but I could feel her staring at me. "It was just a few practical jokes. It's not like we hate you."

"You used to be my friend. And then you got in with Reb and Jennifer. That was the worst part. I never expected the Evil Twins to be nice, but I thought you were."

I felt like Melissa had given me a karate chop on the back of my neck. All along, I'd thought I was the nice one. But then I knew. Reb and Jennifer could have done anything—set Melissa's bed on fire, tied her to an anthill, shaved her head and made her go naked to the dance. None of that was as bad as me making "tinkle, tinkle" jokes after we'd gone canoeing together that day. It was worse. Worse for me to do what I did than anything they could've done to her. Melissa didn't expect them to be nice to her. But she'd thought for a little while that I was her friend.

All I wanted was to be to a triplet. A Terrible Triplet.

Melissa's eyes were boring through my back. I stood there with my back to her, both my feet cemented to the floor. "Want me to help you look for your bracelet?" I asked softly over my shoulder.

"Don't bother."

I didn't turn around to face her.

"Well, I hope you find it."

I walked out the door and headed toward the lake. But I could still feel that karate chop.

# CHAPTER 20

When I finally got back to the lake, morning activities were just ending, and everyone was pulling the canoes ashore.

"What took you so long?" asked Reb. "Did you get lost?"

"Really? I wasn't gone *that* long."

Reb and Jennifer came out of the shed where they'd hung up their paddles. Reb stared at me. "Are you okay?"

"Of course I'm okay. Why wouldn't I be?" Could they tell by looking at me what had just happened? Was my face still red?

Reb shrugged. "I don't know. You just look a little funny."

"I'm fine!" The last thing I needed right now was the third degree.

"Good. Then let's go."

"Go where?"

"Back to the cabin, of course. You know—hang out, wait for lunch. Do what we do pretty much every day." Reb looked at me.

"Oh, yeah. I guess activities are over now." I took a deep breath, trying to act normal. But as we walked to the cabin, my stomach was doing backflips. What if Melissa was still there?

Would she still be in the middle of a nervous break-down? Would she accuse them of stealing her bracelet too? She wouldn't if she knew what was good for her, but she was practically out of her mind right now. Who knew what crazy thing she might try? I couldn't take any more drama. At least not in the next fifteen minutes.

I held my breath and crossed my fingers behind my back. If only I could think of some excuse for us not to go back to the cabin. But I couldn't. Anyway, they'd see right through that, and then they'd be really suspicious, wondering why I was trying to keep them away.

Reb opened the screen door and walked in first, with Jennifer behind her. When the roof didn't blow off and things didn't explode all over the place, I followed them. A quick glance around, and I saw that Molly and Jordan were on Side B, but otherwise no one else was there. I breathed for the first time in ten minutes.

"Hey, guys. What's up?" asked Reb.

"Nothing much," they answered, and since they looked completely normal, I assumed they hadn't seen Melissa crying. All our trunks were closed, and everything looked the way it was supposed to. Whew. I was so relieved I plopped down on my bunk.

"I don't know about you guys, but I need a shower," said Reb. "I smell like a frog." She opened up her trunk to get her stuff. And then she froze. She turned around really slowly and looked at Jennifer and me.

"Somebody's been in my trunk."

My heart sprang up to my mouth. I had to swallow to get it back in my chest where it belonged. I sat up on the edge of my bunk.

"What?" yelled Jennifer, all shocked. I tried to look surprised too.

Reb had this really stunned look on her face. "My stuff is moved."

"How can you tell?" I asked. It was a stupid question, because her trunk is the most organized space in the entire camp. I think she was a drill sergeant in a former life.

"Because my stuff is moved around and out of place. My clothes are rumpled up—someone's been in here."

"Who do you think did it?" asked Jennifer. The worst thing anyone could do was go through your trunk. We didn't have any privacy or any personal space, except for our trunks.

Reb just looked at Jennifer. "Do I even have to say?"

"But why? Did she steal anything?" asked Jennifer, which was a logical question.

Reb turned back, like she hadn't even thought of that. She spent about ten minutes sorting through her stuff very carefully. "I don't think so," she said, all cautious.

If Reb hadn't noticed, I never would've said anything, but she did. I opened my mouth, but the story was stuck way down in my throat, like an old popcorn kernel. I either needed to cough it up or swallow it.

"Oh my gosh, I ought to check my trunk too!" Jennifer yelled all of a sudden. She rushed over and began searching it.

Melissa might as well have left a signed note saying, *While you were out, I searched all your trunks because I think you stole something of mine. Hope you don't mind.*

"I think everything's okay," Jennifer said after examining all her stuff.

Reb looked at me. "You're awfully quiet. What about your trunk?"

"I'm just so shocked she'd be stupid enough to do this," I said.

Then I knelt in front of my trunk and looked through it. "Well, I don't see any obvious clues. It's a mess, like always." It still amazed me that Reb could glance at her trunk and tell immediately that somebody had been through her stuff. I wouldn't notice if a pack of baboons was nesting in my trunk.

"She must have done it this morning. Did you notice anything strange when you came back to change?"

*Yeah. Melissa was scrounging through your trunk like a cop with a search warrant. That was pretty strange.* "Not really," I said.

"I just know Melissa's behind this." Reb shook her head. "We've been doing stuff to her, she probably got mad, and now she's trying to get back at us."

"But nothing is missing," I tried to point out. If I could just convince Reb this wasn't such a big deal, maybe I could prevent a possible murder.

"How do we know she was trying to steal something? She could have been trying to . . . sabotage us. You know, pour shampoo on our clothes or squeeze toothpaste into our shoes." Reb closed her trunk and frowned. "I *hate* people going through my stuff. Especially here at camp where there's no privacy anyway. Anybody who'd do something like that . . ." Reb pressed her lips together. She was beyond mad. She was seething.

"What are we going to do?" Jennifer asked.

"I don't know yet. But we're *not* going to let this go."

I knew we were in for a major battle. But there was nothing I could do. I hadn't coughed up the popcorn kernel. I'd swallowed it. So there was no turning back.

# CHAPTER 21

When afternoon activities started, Reb watched Melissa like a hawk to see where she was going, and without even waiting for me and Jennifer to follow her, she took off after her. Jennifer and I just looked at each other like, *Oh, great. Here we go.*

Melissa walked down Middler Line with Reb right behind her. With Jennifer and me behind Reb, we looked like some weird parade. I could tell by looking at Melissa's back that she knew she was being followed. She walked with her body all tensed, and she'd turn her head a little bit like she wanted to look over her shoulder but didn't dare.

After we passed the lake, I figured out that Melissa was heading to the riflery range. We were on a dirt path that went through the woods, and all around us the locusts were buzzing in the trees. The idea of Reb and Melissa being around lethal weapons made me incredibly nervous.

Then we got to the riflery range. It was just a wooden platform with a roof over the top, kind of hidden in among all the trees. On the platform were bare mattresses for the shooters, who would lie on their stomachs and prop themselves up on their elbows to shoot. Across from the platform were the stands for tacking up the paper targets. There were girls already there shooting, and we could hear the cracking sound the rifles made.

Finally Reb caught up with Melissa and stopped her.

"I need to talk to you, Melissa."

Melissa turned around. The two of them stood on the path, face to face. Jennifer and I were a little behind Reb, keeping quiet. Melissa looked a little nervous, but she also looked kind of defiant, which was a first. "About what?"

"Somebody's been snooping around in our trunks. All our stuff's moved around and messed up. Do you know anything about that?"

Melissa glanced past Reb's shoulder and looked at me. I shook my head very slightly. The look on her face told me she'd gotten my meaning.

"Why are you asking me?"

"Gee—let's see. Somebody was snooping in my trunk, and Jennifer's trunk, and Kelly's trunk. You're the only other person on our side of the cabin. I doubt Rachel or any of the Side B guys did it. I'd say that makes you a prime suspect."

Melissa looked at me again, and I looked back at her. All she had to do was deny everything. Just keep quiet. Not admit to a thing.

"Well, aren't you a real girl detective!" she said, all sarcastic. Jennifer and I looked at each other in shock. Where did mousy Melissa get off with such a gutsy answer? But she wasn't even done.

"It just so happens I've got a mystery of my own. My favorite bracelet is gone. I think somebody stole it. Maybe the Girl Detective can solve that one." Melissa crossed her arms and looked Reb dead in the eye. The pop of rifle fire sounded like firecrackers.

Reb stared at her, obviously not having a clue what she was implying. "SO?"

"Don't you get it? Cabin 1 has two mysteries: your invaded trunks and my missing bracelet. If you solve either one of them, let me know."

Reb looked confused for a second, but then the lightbulb over her head finally went on. "Are you saying you looked in my trunk for your stupid bracelet?"

"It's not stupid. It's very valuable. A family heirloom. It was my grandmother's."

"I don't care if it's Queen Elizabeth's! Did you search my trunk?"

"Did you steal my bracelet?" asked Melissa.

"Are you asking me or accusing me?" said Reb.

"Seems like you're accusing me of trespassing," Melissa shot back.

"Seems like I have a reason to. But there's one big difference here. You've basically admitted going through my stuff. But I didn't steal your bracelet."

"Look, all I care about is getting my bracelet back. You can take anything else of mine. Anything. I don't care. But I've got to have my bracelet." Melissa's voice shook a little, and I thought she was going to start bawling again, but she didn't. "It can't be replaced. I just want you to know that."

"I did not steal your bracelet! Are you going to stand there and say I did?"

"Considering all the things you've done to me, I wouldn't put anything past you, Rebecca Callison. Not even theft."

"You're calling me a *thief*? Is that what I'm hearing?"

Was Melissa shaking? I couldn't tell. Could Reb see

that she was shaking? Melissa put her hands on her hips and looked right at Reb. "Did I stutter?"

Reb was actually stunned. I saw her freeze for a split second. Nobody ever challenged her like that. Ever. But then she recovered.

Reb's voice was a whisper. An unbelievably creepy whisper. "Excuse me, but have we met? Do you even know who I am?"

Just listening to it made me break out in goose bumps, and she wasn't even talking to me. She stepped up to within inches of Melissa's face. They were practically nose to nose. Melissa drew back a fraction, and there was sheer terror in her eyes. But she stood her ground.

"Let me introduce myself," Reb whispered. Slowly, very slowly, she reached down, picked up Melissa's hand, and shook it. "I am your worst nightmare."

And when Reb said that, I knew it was all over. No hope of a peace treaty. She'd formally declared war.

CHAPTER 22

## Wednesday, July 2

After lunch there was a huge stampede, with everyone trying to get through the dining hall doors at the same time. We all wanted to check our little wooden cubby-holes on the dining hall porch for one thing—to see if we got any mail. Every single day I got a huge thrill at this time because I never knew—would I get any mail today?

I'd been pretty lucky all summer. Hardly a day went by when I didn't get at least one letter or e-mail. But when I reached into my mailbox and pulled out an envelope with a Camp Crockett insignia on it, I almost fainted right there on the dining hall porch. Above the insignia was a name printed in ink: Ethan Hurley.

Ethan had written me a letter! My heart was pounding so hard I could barely breathe.

It's kind of stupid, but that moment was one of the happiest in my life. I hadn't even read what he'd said, but right now, the world was absolutely perfect.

Reb and Jennifer came up beside me. I was still in a daze.

"Get any mail?" asked Reb.

I looked at her and Jennifer. "A letter from Ethan. The Camp Crockett guy." I held it up and showed them the envelope, and my hands were actually shaking a little.

"OMIGOD! OMIGOD! OMIGOD!" Jennifer screamed. "Open it!" Everyone turned around and looked at us.

Being very careful not to tear the envelope too much—I didn't want to demolish the first letter I'd ever gotten from a boy—I opened it up and started reading. Jennifer and Reb were breathing down my neck, and I kept moving to keep them from reading over my shoulder.

Hey Kelly—

What's up? I guess you heard we're gonna have another dance on Sat. That's pretty cool, huh? Dustin says he's going to ask Melissa to dance again. What a stud, huh? I was in the doubles

❤ 146 ❤

tennis tournament last week. Me and my partner did pretty good but we got elliminited. Hope your having fun at Pine Haven. Camp's okay but I'm really looking forward to my birthday in August, plus we go on vacation to Hilton Head SC then too. I'll send you a postcard if you give me your home address. See ya Sat.

Ethan

"What'd it say? You are sooo lucky. I hate you," said Jennifer.

Reb was chanting, "Read it! Read it! Read it!"

"You guys, leave me alone. Can't I have any privacy?"

"No, none. We're your sisters. C'mon, you guys always make me read my e-mails from Wes," said Reb, coming up to take the letter out of my hand.

"Okay, fine, but be careful with it! Don't get your grimy fingerprints on it!"

Reb laughed and held up her hands. "Okay—we won't lay our grimy hands on it, but hold it still so we can read it."

So I held the letter for them while they read it. When they'd finished, Jennifer sighed. "Should I write Curtis? Just to let him know I haven't forgotten him?"

"Sure, if you want to," I said, but I never would've had the nerve to write Ethan if he hadn't written me first. "But what should I do now? Should I write him back?" I had to play things just right. I didn't want to screw this up.

"Yeah, definitely," said Reb. "Just to let him know you got it. But keep it casual, like he did. Like, 'Yeah, the next dance is coming up. Guess I'll see you there.' Casual."

Jennifer nodded. "Reb's right. You should write him, but don't make a big deal out of it."

I nodded and sighed. It was a *huge* relief having friends advise me on the next move. I was so glad I had Reb and Jennifer.

Reb grinned at me, hooking her arm around my shoulder. "That's cool he wrote you. It's definitely a sign he likes you."

I tried not to smile as I carefully folded the letter and put it back in its envelope. "You guys will help me figure out what to say?"

"Absolutely."

All during rest hour, I lay on my bunk and scribbled out different drafts of letters to Ethan. I figured Jennifer was working on a letter on the top bunk to her Camp Crockett guy too, because I could actually hear her pen scratching on paper. Melissa was on her cot, her back to the rest of us. She seemed to be napping, but maybe she was faking it so she didn't have to look at us.

Reb was lying flat on her back, staring up at the rafters. That was weird. She wasn't preparing herself for Harvard or Yale, like usual. Since yesterday, Reb had become totally obsessed with how to get back at Melissa. Things had gotten even more tense. Yesterday Melissa had told Rachel about her missing bracelet, and Rachel gave the three of us the third degree. Reb was furious.

"Give me a lie detector test! Get me a stack of Bibles to swear on!" she'd yelled. I wasn't sure if Rachel believed us or not. She'd made us all search the cabin—under the bunks, in the corners, behind all our trunks. But of course we didn't find the bracelet.

All of a sudden Reb sat up with a big grin on her face and got a pad of paper out of her trunk. Was she going to help me write my letter? Or work algebra problems?

"What're you doing?" I whispered, but Rachel shushed me.

Reb had this excited look on her face. "I've got it!" she whispered back. Another shush from Rachel. If we said anything else, she'd keep us ten extra minutes after rest hour. She was a regular slave driver at times.

When the bell rang, Melissa sat up, put her shoes on, and left. She'd definitely been faking. I knew she was still really upset about her bracelet. But what could we do? We hadn't done anything.

Jennifer and I waited for Reb, but she still sat cross-legged on her cot, writing away.

"Okay, ladies. Out the door. You'll be late for afternoon activities," said Rachel.

"I gotta finish this letter to my mommy. I'm telling her what an inspiration and role model you are, and obviously that takes a long time," Reb answered, not looking up from her paper.

"Move it. Out the door. Rest hour's over." Rachel was afraid that if she left us in the cabin, we'd cut activities and wind up cabin-sitting.

"All done!" Reb announced happily. She folded up the paper and stuffed it into her shorts pocket.

We walked down Middler Line in the crowd of girls, but Reb said she needed to stop in Solitary. When she came out, she looked around and said, "Let's go back and get our tennis rackets. We forgot them."

But obviously we weren't going back for our rackets. By now the cabin was empty. Reb plopped down on her cot and looked up at Jennifer and me with that same huge grin on her face.

"Kelly's love letter got me thinking. I know what we're going to do to Melissa."

Reb pulled the folded papers out of her pocket and looked up to make sure she had our attention. Then she cleared her throat and started reading:

Dear Dustin,

I bet you're surprised to get a letter from me. I can't believe I'd ever be brave enough to write to a guy, but here goes. You may have gotten the idea that I didn't like you. Well, you're wrong. With the next dance coming up, you're all I've been thinking about. Although I'm practically dying of embarrassment telling you all this, I really like you. But when we were slow dancing, I was so nervous I could barely talk to you.

I know I walked away and left you standing there, and I feel so stupid. But that was my first slow dance, and I was a little nervous about it. I'm hoping to see you Saturday, and maybe we can dance again. And this time, during a slow dance, I promise I won't walk away. Maybe we can go out on the porch. The counselors here always joke about being on Porch Patrol, but they can't watch us every second. I've never kissed a boy, but I'm hoping that will change. Soon.

See you Saturday.

Love,
Melissa Bledsoe

Jennifer shook her head in amazement. "Are you really going to mail that?"

"Of course! Isn't this the *perfect* revenge? I knew I'd come up with something. I just didn't know it would be this good."

Jennifer looked in the mirror and said to her reflection, "I would die if somebody sent a letter like that to a boy from me. I don't know which is worse—sending it to a boy you like or to one you can't stand."

"Melissa would never write a letter like that," I pointed out. Reb couldn't seriously be thinking about sending it. This was way too much.

"I know that. But how does Dustin know that?"

"What do you think he'll do when he gets the letter?" wondered Jennifer.

"At the dance he'll be all over her. He'll make her night miserable!"

"I don't know, Reb. It's almost too much. Haven't we done enough to her already?" I asked.

"Too much? *Too much?* I'll tell you what was too much. Going through our trunks was too much. Calling us thieves and liars right to our faces was too much. Telling Rachel we had something to do with her missing bracelet was too much. You think this is too much? Hey, the way I see it, I'm letting her off easy."

I was actually kind of scared of Reb at that moment. Her face was all red and flushed. She looked mad at *me*. I kept quiet.

Reb looked at me steadily. "We're together on this, aren't we? We're triplets, right?" She held up her wristband to remind me. She usually thought the whole wristband thing was stupid, but now of course it was all for one, and one for all.

What could I say to that? The one thing I'd learned was how hard it was to say no to Reb.

"We'll always be triplets," said Jennifer, holding out her arm to show her wristband. I nodded and held out mine, too. But I felt like a traitor. The weird thing was, I felt like a traitor to everyone—Reb, Jennifer, and Melissa. But who was I betraying? I couldn't betray everyone at the same time. So who was it?

Reb seemed satisfied. She looked around. "Remember that personalized paper we saw when we were short-sheeting her? Let's use some of that." She found the stack of paper on the shelf by Melissa's bed. It had a border of little purple flowers around it, and across the top in type like cursive handwriting it said, "From Melissa."

"Perfect! Absolutely perfect!" Reb took a couple of sheets off the stack. "She probably won't miss these," she added with a grin. Then she sat cross-legged on her cot while she copied the letter onto Melissa's stationery. It was so believable this way, with Melissa's name on it. But then, that's the way Reb wanted it.

When she was done, she looked up at us. "Okay, if we mail it tomorrow, Dustin should get it Friday. He won't have time to write her back, but he'll have plenty of time to think about her before the dance on Saturday." She nodded her head, all satisfied that this was going to work great. "This is going to be the best revenge ever!"

## CHAPTER 23

### Saturday, July 5

"Does my hair look okay?" Jennifer asked again. It was the fifth time at least.

"No, it looks terrible. You really oughta go to the bathroom and fix it," I snapped.

Jennifer winced. "Jeez, what's with you?"

"Look, I'm sorry. I've told you it looks fine. Would you please stop asking?"

It wasn't her fault. We were all waiting in the dining hall for the Crockett boys to walk in. I was a nervous wreck. Reb, on the other hand, was absolutely cool and calm. She'd set her trap. Now all she had to do was sit back and watch.

But I didn't want to watch. I didn't want any part of it.

All day yesterday, I'd wanted to tell Melissa about the letter. But the day was all weird because of the Fourth of July. We didn't have any regular activities. We had a capture-the-flag game in the morning and a counselor hunt in the afternoon. Then everybody went skinny-dipping, and for dinner we ate hot dogs and ice cream outside on the hill and watched fireworks over the lake.

It should've been fun, but I kept walking up behind Melissa and then not doing anything. It was horrible. It was like needing to sneeze, but not being able to. I wanted to tell her. I just couldn't get it out. I'd be standing right by her, and I'd think, *Hey, Melissa*. But nothing ever came out. Plus Reb and Jennifer were always close by.

Anyway, maybe it was better *not* to tell her. Maybe nothing would happen. Maybe Dustin wouldn't do anything. Maybe Melissa would never even find out. If nothing happened, then it would be better if she never even knew the letter existed.

When the boys walked in, everybody got all excited. Right away I saw Ethan in the crowd. Should I walk up to him? Or wait for him to see me? Luckily he saw me and kind of waved. But then he just stood there talking to some guys.

Okay, what was up? Did I sound stupid in my letter?

Was he leading me on? What should I do? But then he walked toward me. Whew. I'd die if he ignored me.

"Hi, how ya doing?" he said. He was wearing an over-size striped polo and cargo shorts with big pockets. His hair looked even blonder than before.

"Good. I got your letter," I said, which was like the stupidest thing in the world to say, because I'd written him back. Obviously he already knew I'd gotten his letter.

"Yeah, I got yours, too."

"Cool. I wasn't sure if it would get there in time." Why was everything out of my mouth sounding absolutely ridiculous? I hadn't been this nervous at the first dance.

"Yeah, it did—yesterday. Thanks for writing back."

Then we didn't say anything for a few awkward, long moments, since we'd completely used up that topic of conversation.

"Oh, hey! Guess who else got a letter—Dustin! Melissa wrote *him* a letter!"

I cringed. Was this stupid letter going to ruin my evening with Ethan? "Oh. He told you about it?"

"Told us about it? He made us all read it about a hundred times. He wouldn't shut up about this Pine Haven babe who's in love with him. Nobody could believe it."

"Really?" I paused for a second. Should I tell him?

He'd find out eventually. "Can you keep a secret?" I asked. It gave me an excuse to lean close to him. He smelled like Axe, and from now on, whenever I smelled that, I would always think of Ethan Hurley. "The letter's a fake. We wrote it."

"*You* wrote it!" he yelled.

"Shhh!" I grabbed his arm. I loved having an excuse to grab his arm. "Keep it down! Reb wrote it. It was her idea." Might as well give credit where credit was due.

"But the sheet of paper said 'Melissa' and everything."

"Yeah. We lifted some of her personalized stationery to make it look legitimate."

"Wow! You guys are too evil!" Ethan marveled. "It did seem unbelievable that a girl would be so crazy about Dustin." He looked at me and nodded admiringly.

"Here you are! Do you want to miss *everything*?" Reb almost knocked us over when she ran up to us. "Dustin's going to move in on Melissa any second now!"

"But Reb, this is *your* project. I'm not going to spend the whole evening following Melissa and Dustin around. Why don't you get Jennifer?"

"Jennifer won't let what's-his-face out of her sight. It's me and you on this."

"Hey, and me!" said Ethan. "Kelly told me about it.

That's amazing! And Dustin fell for it. We all did. The whole cabin really thought Melissa wrote him."

Reb's eyes lit up. "You mean he told all his friends about it? Perfect! Things are going even better than I planned! Look—there's Melissa."

She was standing by some other girls, and Dustin was a few feet away. He'd obviously seen her, and now it looked like he was working up the nerve to go up to her. Finally he walked up, put his arm around her back, and tapped her on the far shoulder. She actually turned to the other side to see who it was, then looked around to see him standing next to her.

Melissa didn't say a word to him. But Dustin was talking. She kind of nodded, like she was listening to him jabber away. Then they started to dance. I couldn't believe it. She'd dance with this guy after what he did the last time? Maybe because all the songs now were fast. He wouldn't have a chance to grab her.

"Why don't *we* dance too?" I asked Ethan.

"You can't take off now," Reb protested. "Things are just getting started."

"Reb, I'm not going to watch their every move all night just in case Dustin burps in her face or something. There's nothing to see now."

"Just don't let them out of your sight. I'll be

watching them too," Reb told us.

At least we were dancing. It ought to give Reb some satisfaction that she'd managed to get Dustin and Melissa together too. Maybe if they danced a few dances together, she'd call it even. And then Melissa would never even know about the letter.

After a few songs, I'd almost forgotten about Melissa and Dustin. I was having a great time with Ethan, just like before. Then Reb came up behind us and grabbed me.

"Let's go. They're at the refreshment table now."

"Really? Let's go see which flavor cookie she picks out—chocolate chip or shortbread."

"Seriously. We need to go over there. Something's about to happen."

I rolled my eyes. "Reb, what do you expect? You think Dustin's gonna tear her clothes off? Or is Melissa gonna spit in his eye? They're *together*. What more do you want? Why do you think something else is going to happen?"

Reb just smiled at me. "Because I'm going to make it happen."

CHAPTER 24

Ethan looked at me. "Come on. Let's see what she's up to."

Reb walked right up to Dustin and Melissa, standing by the refreshment table. Ethan and I went up too and got some drinks. Melissa obviously hated this guy. She looked like she just wanted to get away from him. Dustin didn't look too thrilled either. Melissa had been so crazy about him in "her" letter, and now she'd turned into a cold fish. If Reb expected some excitement from these two, I figured she'd be disappointed.

"Hey, Melissa, how's it going?" Reb asked, all friendly. But not in the tone she usually used with Melissa. She really sounded nice this time. Melissa tensed up when Reb approached her. She had the look she always had with Reb—like she was ready to break and run if Reb pounced on her. Obviously, she was suspicious that her worst nightmare suddenly wanted to have a chat with her.

Reb leaned close to Melissa. "So, are you having a good time?"

Melissa looked at her cautiously, then looked back at Dustin. "Not really."

Reb looked surprised. "Not really? But you two have been together all night. I think you make a cute couple."

Melissa looked nauseated. "I can't stand him. I want to get away from him."

Reb smiled at Ethan and me. "Well, if you don't like him, you shouldn't have written him that love letter."

Melissa looked at her. "I didn't write him."

"Oh, c'mon. Don't be embarrassed. Kelly wrote Ethan, too. It's no big deal to write a boy. But you really led Dustin on, Melissa. You shouldn't have written all that stuff if you don't really like him."

"What are you talking about?"

"Ethan says Dustin let everybody in the cabin read it. Oh, and your 'Melissa' stationery? What a sweet touch that was."

Melissa froze. She looked at me, then at Ethan, then back at Reb. "My stationery?" She looked over at Dustin, still standing by the refreshment table stuffing a cookie in his mouth. "What did you *do*?"

"It was your letter. Don't you remember all the stuff you wrote to Dustin? It was just a couple of days ago. Have you forgotten already?"

Melissa was about to walk off. Then she stopped and looked at Reb. "What did you . . . ? Tell me what you did." I could see tears welling up in her eyes.

Reb looked at Ethan. "Melissa can't seem to remember what she said. But Dustin read it to your whole cabin. So, Ethan. Do you remember any good parts?"

"Uh, yeah. I think I do." Ethan went right along like he and Reb had planned this for weeks. "You said something about how the Porch Patrol can't watch us every second. And you were hoping for your first kiss."

Melissa stood there with her arms crossed, trying to look tough, or mad, or something. "So. You wrote that guy a letter and signed my name to it. And you did it on my stationery. Very funny. Ha, ha." It was a good strategy to act like she didn't really care. It might have worked, if it hadn't been for the tears that she just couldn't stop. Melissa was about to turn and run, and I wanted to grab her and make her stay. I knew I had to stop her. I had to keep her from running away in tears.

And then something happened inside me. It felt like

jumping off the high dive. Something inside me said, *Okay, go*. My breath flew out of me and my stomach rose up inside me and I was flying through space, waiting to land. But I had jumped.

"That's not what happened," I said. I walked over to Dustin and grabbed him. "That letter you got from Melissa? She didn't write it. It was a fake," I said in front of him, Ethan, Melissa, Reb, God, and everybody else.

"Kelly!" Reb yelled. But I kept going.

"Melissa didn't write it. I wrote it."

Now everything was in fast-forward. Reb was grabbing me, trying to pull me away, trying to get me to shut up. Dustin was about to choke on his chocolate chip cookies. Melissa had stopped crying and was just standing there, caught in the headlights. I had no idea what Ethan was doing. It felt like everybody around us was watching us. Maybe they were. Maybe it just felt that way.

"I wrote it!" I was yelling. It seemed like I said that about fifty times. It seemed like I'd been shouting that all night.

"Kelly, SHUT UP!" Reb also yelled that a lot.

I don't remember everything too well. It was pretty out of control. At some point Dustin said, "I don't believe you. It had her name right on it!"

"I took some of her stationery to make it look real."

"You're lying!"

"Shut up!"

"Then ask her. Ask her what it said. She doesn't know, because she never even saw it!"

"What'd it say?"

"I don't know! I didn't write it," Melissa insisted.

"Shut up!"

"It starts off, 'I bet you're surprised to get a letter from me. I can't believe I'd have the nerve to write a guy, but here goes. . . .'"

"Maybe she read it to you before she mailed it."

"But she didn't! She didn't know anything about it! I took her stationery! I wrote it! I mailed it!"

"Shut up! *Shut up!*" A hand kept trying to cover up my mouth. Reb's, I guess, but for some reason I kept thinking it was Ethan's. "It was a joke! It was just a stupid practical joke! I'm sorry." I said that to everybody. To Melissa, Dustin, Reb. Everyone.

"SHUT UP!" Reb roared in my face. Would she slap me? She might have. But somebody dragged us out the door. Was it Ethan? Jennifer?

It was Rachel.

"Girl fight!" A loud meowing noise. Then laughing. Out the door, on the porch, out in the gravel beside the dining hall. Not even dark yet. How could it not even be dark yet?

"*What* . . . is the problem?"

Reb and me standing there. Like we were about to box. Breathing so hard. Both of us. Her face so red. Was my face that red? It felt hot. Where was Ethan? Was Jennifer out here too? People were watching us from the porch. The outside air felt so cool.

"You ruined it! You ruined everything!" yelled Reb.

"Calm down. What's this all about?" asked Rachel.

"I'm sorry! Look, I'm sorry, okay? I'm sorry. It just went too far," I said.

"It was perfect! You ruined it!"

"You guys settle down, or I'll send you to the cabin and you'll miss the rest of the dance. I'll take you there myself," said Rachel.

"It just needed to stop! It had to stop! I didn't blame you."

"I HATE YOU! GOD! I HATE YOU! NO FRIEND HAS EVER TURNED ON ME LIKE THAT!"

Lightning bugs were coming out of the grass. Crickets were chirping.

A beautiful summer evening.

I wished I was anywhere else but here.

## CHAPTER 25

## Monday, July 7

I couldn't believe how beautiful the view was from up here. I was sitting on a bench on the porch of Middler Lodge. In the distance I could see the blue misty mountains, and in front of them were dark green mountains. Then there was a strip of mountains that were light green from the sunlight. Above the mountains, the sky was a pale blue with soft, cotton-ball clouds. Too bad I didn't have my camera.

I could hear Molly and Jordan talking inside the lodge because the big wooden doors were open. Melissa was in there too. Rachel and Tis had sent us all down here before dinner to plan for the talent show coming up in a few days. Every cabin had to enter at least one act, and even though we all swore we were completely untalented, they made us come down here anyway. Brittany and Erin got out of it because they were packing to go on the hiking honor trip tomorrow with Rachel and all the other superhikers. Honor trips were for people who'd worked really hard and done very well at one activity.

I had no idea where Reb and Jennifer were. Jennifer and I were still wearing our wristbands. But what was the point? Reb had stopped wearing hers. On Sunday morning I'd seen her take it off and toss it into her trunk like, *I'm done with that*.

We weren't triplets anymore.

On Saturday Reb and I never went back to the dance. I didn't get to see Ethan, but in some ways that was good. I'd probably never see him again. That made me really sad. He was supposed to write me from Hilton Head too. But I never had a chance to give him my home address. Who knew what he thought of me now? He probably laughed about our "cat fight" with all his friends afterward. Maybe he didn't. I hope he didn't.

After our huge fight, Rachel took us both back to the cabin. She tried to get us to talk, but neither one of us would tell her anything. By that time I was crying. Reb didn't cry. She sat on her cot with her back to us and refused to say a word.

"Is this over some boy?" asked Rachel.

"No," I said, wiping the tears away. "Well, kind of." It was easier just to lie about it.

"Well, no boy is worth losing a friend over. You two are best friends. You have to work this out."

I nodded and glanced over at Reb's back. Was I really Reb's best friend? I always thought Jennifer was and I was her second-best friend. I'd always wanted to be in first place.

Rachel left us alone because she had to go back to the dance. She probably thought it would give us a chance to make up.

Reb sat on her bed with her back to me, not moving. She was a statue.

"Would you please talk to me?" I said in this really whimpering, teary voice. I wished I could stop crying. She hated people being all weak and wimpy.

She just got up and walked out the door. I had no idea where she went that night. But I know she didn't go back to the dance, because I asked Jennifer about it later and she said she never saw her.

Since Saturday night Reb had not said one single word to me. Even though we slept five feet away from each other and ate at the same table together, I had become invisible.

I could hear Jordan and Molly inside the lodge talking.

"No, I got it. How about this?" Jordan was saying.

"You know, you're really good at this," said Molly. They were probably annoyed that I was sitting out here and not participating. But they knew Reb and I were in the middle of a huge fight.

"What do you think, Melissa?"

"I liked it the second way. That's the best one."

"Kelly?"

Without even turning around, I could tell it was Melissa.

"Mind if I come out?"

I looked over my shoulder and shrugged, like I didn't care what she did. She came out on the porch and stood by the railing.

"Um, I just wanted to thank you. For standing up for me."

I rolled my eyes. "Yeah, no sweat."

"No, honestly—thanks. I really appreciate it. I thought it was really brave. The way you took the blame. In front of everyone. Because I know *you* didn't write it."

I just shrugged. I really did not want to talk about this. Couldn't she tell? I was not trying to be brave. I've never been brave. I've never taken the blame for any-thing in my life. Even stuff I *was* guilty of. That was the weird part. It was so unlike me. I just didn't want to blame Reb.

"I know Reb did it. You couldn't be so mean. She did everything, and you and Jennifer just went along with her. Like with everything else. She was always the one who did everything. She's the meanest person I've ever met in my entire life."

I just sat there, fiddling with my wristband. I won-dered when I should take it off.

"So are you and Reb still mad at each other?"

"What do you think?"

"Well, you're better off. Some friend she is to turn on you like that. I guess you see that now. I'd rather have a scorpion for a friend than Reb Callison."

"Melissa, shut up! You think losing my best friend makes me better off? Reb hates me now, and it's all your fault!"

Melissa drew back. "My fault?"

"Yes, your fault. If you'd had a spine, you would have stood up for *yourself*. Why didn't you ever stand up for yourself? That's why Reb kept picking on you."

"You were the ones who wrote the letter! I didn't even know anything about it!"

"If you hadn't gone through our trunks, Reb never would've written that letter! Can't you just face the fact that *you* lost your bracelet, and we had nothing to do with it?"

Melissa's mouth hung open. "I just . . . all I was trying to do was thank you. . . ."

"Fine! You've done that! Now can't you leave me alone?"

Melissa backed away. "Why are you so mad at *me*? I was hoping we could be friends. . . ."

"We can't be friends!" I yelled at her. "I only did that at the dance because I felt sorry for you. Rescuing you cost me *my* best friend. That was too high a price to pay. If I had it to do over, I'd keep my mouth shut!"

Melissa backed through the open doors to the lodge. "You're just as bad as Reb!"

"What happened?" I could hear Molly and Jordan asking her.

Mumble, mumble, mumble. Somebody came to the door and looked at me, but I didn't turn around.

"Well, we've got to finish this." Blah, blah, blah. Thank God Jordan and Molly had discovered some hidden talent.

I felt bad for yelling at Melissa. I hadn't meant to; it all just came spurting out like soda from a shaken-up can. It wasn't really her fault. We did pick on her. But they were just pranks. At first. Then it got worse. If she hadn't searched all our trunks and called us all thieves, things wouldn't have gone this far.

Was that true, what I said? If I had it to do over, would I keep my mouth shut?

I honestly didn't know the answer to that.

# 26

## Tuesday, July 8

It was time to end this. This silent treatment stuff was kind of understandable for the first day or two, when we were both still so upset and mad, but we couldn't go on like this forever. This was the last week of camp.

I made up my mind. I'd be the first to break the ice. When morning activities started, I followed Reb. Jennifer saw what I was up to and caught up with me.

"Hey, where ya going?"

"I'm gonna try to talk to Reb."

Jennifer sniffed. "Good luck. I've tried talking to her, but she just won't open up. I've never seen her like this. I know she feels really, really bad about all this. I can tell she wants us all to be friends again."

"Really?" I was surprised, because that sure wasn't

the impression I was getting. Reb treated me like I was invisible. "Then maybe it'll help if I make the first move?"

Jennifer frowned. "I don't know. You know how she can be. You want my theory?"

I nodded.

Jennifer leaned close to me, talking just above a whisper. "I think she's embarrassed. That's why she's not talking to anyone, always doing things alone now. That's why she avoids me and won't even look at you."

"Embarrassed about what?" I didn't get it. Reb sure didn't act embarrassed to me. She seemed mad. I got the feeling she really hated me.

"That she went too far with the whole letter thing. And that she got so mad at you. She's embarrassed about the way she acted, Kelly. But you know how she is. She's so proud, so afraid to ever let down her guard and admit she's not absolutely perfect about everything. She'd rather walk barefoot across hot coals than admit she made a mistake."

"Then it will help if I try to talk to her," I said.

Jennifer shrugged. "Maybe." But she didn't sound very convinced. "Want me to come with you?"

I shook my head. "Thanks, but . . . it's kind of just between me and Reb. You don't mind, do you?" I didn't want to leave Jennifer out, but I did feel like I needed to talk to Reb alone.

"No. I know what you mean. Just tell me what happens, okay?"

After Jennifer walked away, I caught up with Reb. I was really nervous.

"Hey. Can I talk to you for a second?" My heart was actually pounding.

Reb stopped walking, but she didn't turn around.

"Are we . . . are you never going to talk to me again?" She just stood there and didn't say anything.

"I'm sorry. I told you that the other night. I'm sorry I messed up your whole revenge against Melissa. Maybe I should've just stayed out of it." If Jennifer was right, if Reb was embarrassed, maybe it would help if I apologized.

"Can't we be friends again? I said I was sorry."

Reb still hadn't turned around. She didn't seem embarrassed. She seemed mad. She wouldn't even look at me. Maybe Jennifer read her all wrong.

"You know," I went on, feeling like a complete idiot, "Saturday's the last day of camp. Then we all leave. And we won't see each other till next year. If all of us even come back next year."

The more silent Reb was, the more I felt I had to

talk to fill up the empty space. I felt like there was one right thing I could say that would put everything back the way it was. That would make us friends again. I just wasn't sure what that one right thing was. But I guess I figured that if I kept talking, maybe I'd hit on it, by accident.

"I want us to be friends again."

Finally Reb turned around. She looked right at me, for the first time in days. But she didn't say anything. She just stood there, silent.

"Can we?" I asked.

"Leave me alone."

Then she walked away.

I don't know how long I stood there.

I watched her walk away. She didn't ever turn around. I felt like a cartoon character who'd just been hit with an anvil. I was flattened. But I couldn't throw the anvil off and pop back to my normal size. It was like I could feel a real weight on my chest crushing me, squeezing all the air out of me.

*That's it*, I kept thinking. *It's over.*

I started to walk. I couldn't see anything around me—no trees or grass or anything. My legs moved, but I had no control over them. I didn't know where they were taking me. I didn't care. Good thing that legs will work like that sometimes, that they'll take you some-place and you don't have to think about it. Somehow I was on the road that went past the camp store and down to the riding stables.

Then, for some reason, I veered off and started walking through the trees till I was away from the road. I didn't want anyone to see me. I didn't want to see anyone. I wished that I was the only person in the whole world.

I eventually stopped walking and found a flat rock to sit on. I don't know how long I sat there. I don't know when I started crying. I honestly don't know if I was there for ten minutes or two hours.

I couldn't believe it was over. Jennifer had read it all wrong. Reb wasn't embarrassed about anything. She just hated me, that's all.

I tried to hate her, too. What was her problem? She *was* kind of mean.

What was I saying? She was incredibly mean. If you weren't her friend.

But before all this happened, she'd never been mean to me. Even when camp first started and she didn't even know me. She was nice to me. Nice to me, mean to Melissa. I'd been so freaking relieved that it'd worked out that way, that she'd chosen me as a friend. And then we started picking on Melissa. Was that the only thing that bonded us together? If we stopped picking on Melissa, was that the end of our friendship?

Melissa was right about Reb being the meanest person she knew. But she was wrong about one thing. *I'd rather have a scorpion for a best friend than Reb Callison.*

Not true. Reb was a good best friend.

Or at least she had been.

She tried to teach me to whistle, helped me with my serve. She read the letter I wrote to Ethan and gave me advice on it. She let me borrow clothes for the dance. A really good friend. It wasn't just picking on Melissa that made us friends. There was more to it than that.

This was my worst nightmare.

I put my head down on my folded-up knees and cried and cried and cried. I cried till I thought I was going to throw up. I cried till I was shuddering every time I breathed in. I cried till I was just so *tired* that I finally stopped.

I sat up and wiped my runny nose on my shirt. I still had on my wristband. I should take that stupid thing off. We even swam and showered with them on, because they were made of that rubbery material.

I slipped the wristband off my wrist. The ink where Jennifer had written "Terrible Triplets" had faded, but I could still read it. I drew my hand back, ready to toss the wristband into the woods. But I didn't. I looked at it for a while, then I slipped it into the pocket of my shorts. Maybe Reb would notice I wasn't wearing mine anymore and feel bad. But then maybe she wouldn't even care. She was done with me.

Even though I was absolutely miserable, it was nice out here in the woods, sitting on this rock. It was all shady and cool under the trees. And birds were flittering about in the branches and making little noises. Everything was so quiet. I could hear people's voices every now and then, but from really far away. After a while I even heard the bell ringing, way off in the distance.

I didn't move. Was it the bell for lunch? Or just the end of morning activities?

Then I made a decision. I'd stay here. I wouldn't show up for lunch, and I'd still be gone by rest hour. Eventually, everybody would realize I was missing.

Then they'd be worried. The counselors would ask everyone when they saw me last. Everyone would start searching the camp. They'd never think to look out here for me. If people came around, I'd duck in the bushes and hide. Maybe I'd even stay out here all night. It was warm enough. It's not like I'd die or anything. Maybe in the middle of the night, I could sneak back to the dining hall and steal food.

At some point they'd have to call in the police. Maybe they'd drag the lake, thinking I might've drowned. They'd bring in search dogs. Big German shepherds and bloodhounds, barking and pulling on their leashes. Rachel would go through my laundry bag and give them a piece of clothing I'd worn. Hopefully a shirt and not something embarrassing like underwear.

Reb would feel really bad. She'd be organizing all the search parties. She'd be wringing her hands and crying. "If I could just talk to her," she'd say. She'd make everyone keep looking long into the night. "We've got to find her! She's my best friend!"

Yep, that was the plan. That's what I decided to do.

# CHAPTER 27

I lay there in the dark, listening to all the night sounds. Frogs were croaking like crazy. All the little tadpoles that were in the lake when camp first started had grown tiny arms and legs a couple of weeks ago, and then they'd lost their tails, and pretty soon they were just little frogs. Frogs make a lot of noise at night.

I was glad it was dark. Nobody could see me. Everyone else was quiet too. I could hear Jennifer rolling around above me. Usually we all whisper a little after lights out, but lately we'd stopped doing that.

I heard Reb sniff in the cot next to me. Was she crying? Doubtful. She probably just had a stuffy nose.

I didn't stay out in the woods, obviously. I didn't even stay there till lunch. I got hungry. Plus, after a while it got kind of boring and I started feeling all itchy, like I was getting chigger or mosquito bites. At lunch everyone acted like things were completely normal. None of them realized how close they'd come to having some major drama over a missing camper.

I let out a sigh, then wished I hadn't. Had Reb heard it? One reason this was so hard to deal with was the fact that we live with each other. It's not like back home. At home, if you have a fight with a friend, you can avoid each other for a while. But at camp everyone eats together, dresses together, sleeps together. There's no avoiding each other.

That's why we all got to be such good friends so fast. It really is like sisters. It's just all so *intense.*

I heard Melissa sit up. I could see her profile in the dark. Then she plopped back down again. Was she asleep? I did feel bad for her. Every free minute she had, she looked for her bracelet. She'd taken everything out of her trunk and searched through it dozens of times.

At lunch we sang this song,

> *Five more days of vacation, back to civilization,*
> *Back to father and mother, back to sister and*
> *brother,*

*Back to sweetheart and lo-uh-ver!*
*I don't want to go home!*

"Five more days!" Molly had groaned. "I can't believe camp will be over in five more days. I'm so depressed, I can't think about it!"

"I know," Melissa said with a sigh. I looked at her, and she must have seen me. "I have five more days to find my bracelet. Then it's lost forever."

Reb had eaten her grilled cheese sandwich like she hadn't heard any of it. That stupid bracelet. None of this would've happened if it weren't for Melissa's missing bracelet. Okay—maybe she was sort of justified for suspecting us. She'd probably always blame us. She'd probably go home and tell her mom that these girls picked on her all the time and stole her grandmother's bracelet. She'd never accept the fact that she'd lost it. She said she never took it off, but obviously she did. Maybe it just fell off. Maybe the catch on it broke. Once the setting fell out of my mom's wedding ring. Just one day it was there, and then the next day it was gone. She never found that, either. Boy, did that cause a lot of drama.

How could I ever get Melissa to believe me? Whatever. Let her go on thinking we did it. I didn't even care anymore.

# CHAPTER 28

## Wednesday, July 9

When I woke up, it took a few seconds for the dream to come back to me. Reb, Jennifer, and I were all talking. Reb had something in her hand. I knew it was Melissa's bracelet, even though I never saw it. Reb was smiling.

"Okay, who wants to do it?" she asked.

"I will," I said. The one thing I remember about that part was how happy Reb was and how glad I was to be her friend.

Then I was kneeling in front of my trunk, and I was afraid Melissa would come in and catch me so I was moving really fast. I was really nervous and excited. I opened my trunk, and there was this little secret compartment in the side of it. It was like my wooden jewelry box at home, the way the lid opened up. But in the dream, it was actually built right into the inside of my trunk. I put the bracelet in there, then closed it up. I was so glad it was hidden. There was no way anyone could tell a secret compartment was there.

Then Reb and I were together. "Good job!" She was so happy with me.

"She'll never find it," I told her.

Omigosh! What a freaky dream!

I looked around. The light was gray. I could barely see. But it wasn't dark any more. It was just starting to get light outside. Everyone was still sound asleep.

I tried to go back to sleep too, but I never did. I lay in bed, rolling around. When the rising bell rang and I was getting dressed, I actually looked around inside my trunk for a secret compartment.

There wasn't one.

After breakfast Reb took off to tennis by herself. Jennifer and I went to the climbing tower. Poor Jennifer. She'd tried talking to Reb too. "I hate that we're not triplets any more!" she kept saying. She was the only one who still wore the wristband. But all her attempts to play peacekeeper failed. Reb just didn't want to talk to anyone.

I felt so depressed at the climbing tower. It reminded me of that first afternoon when we all hung out together.

Everything was different this week anyway. Camp was winding down. Lots of people were gone on honor trips as a reward for working really hard at one activity, and the counselors didn't care anymore whether we just goofed off.

"I know Reb feels really bad that you guys aren't friends anymore."

I looked down at Jennifer, who was a few feet under me. "Did she say that?"

"Well, no. But I can tell she's thinking that. I think she's depressed."

I shook my head in disbelief. "She's not depressed. She just hates me."

"Oh yeah? Then why won't she talk to me, either? She doesn't hate *me*. I'm telling you—she's miserable, but she just doesn't know how to fix things."

"I don't believe that for a minute. We've both tried talking to her. If she wanted to fix things, she should've just talked back."

"This may sound weird, but I think not talking to anyone is her way of punishing herself."

"I doubt that." All I knew was that camp was almost over. And if things didn't get better soon, they'd never be resolved.

Jennifer and I didn't go all the way to the top. We slid

down our safety ropes and unstrapped our harnesses.

"I had the weirdest dream last night." That dream had been haunting me all morning. I couldn't get it out of my head. I hate dreams like that, that you can't forget about. That you can still *feel*, late in the day, long after you've woken up.

I told Jennifer my dream, and I even admitted to her that I'd looked for the secret compartment. She laughed at that part. The one thing about the dream that I really still felt was what good friends Reb and I were, and how happy we both were.

"Maybe it means I should look in my trunk," I said. "I mean, what if it is in there? By accident? What if it fell in there or something and I never even knew it?"

Jennifer looked skeptical. "Maybe."

"Maybe I should go back to the cabin and take all my stuff out. . . ." I stopped dead still, absolutely frozen.

Jennifer stopped and looked at me. "What?"

I could barely breathe, I was so excited.

"*What?* What's wrong?"

I still couldn't speak. It hit me. Just like a bolt of lightning.

"Kelly! What is wrong?"

"Jennifer." I grabbed her by the shoulders. "I think I know where to look for it."

# CHAPTER 29

In a flash we were back in the cabin. Nobody else was there. The whole way back Jennifer kept begging, "Will you tell me?" But I wouldn't. I was afraid to say it. Afraid I'd jinx it.

"Okay, where? Where?" she asked, now that we were back. I had a few places that I wanted to look. First in the cabin, and if not there, then one other place.

I walked over to where raincoats and a few other clothes were hanging on the metal rod over the beds. Hanging up with all the other stuff was one item I wanted to check. Melissa's white bathrobe.

"Oh!" Jennifer exclaimed, as I pulled the robe off the wire hanger. I dug inside one pocket. Nothing. I was almost afraid to reach inside the other. I put my hand inside and felt around.

Nothing.

I looked inside both pockets. Nothing. I shook the bathrobe. Nothing.

I felt this incredible sinking feeling. Jennifer stood there with her arms crossed. "Well, it was a good idea."

I looked around at Melissa's shelves. "There's a few more places," I said. On the wooden shelf by Melissa's bed was a stack of baby blue bath towels. When Jennifer saw where I was heading, she actually sucked in her breath.

I picked up the first towel and carefully unfolded it. Nothing! There were four more. With each one I unfolded, I felt more and more disappointed. If it wasn't here, there was still one other place to look. Around the shower stalls. I picked up the last towel and unfolded it and was just about to put it back down when I saw something.

A glint.

I turned the towel over. There, on the other side of it, was a bracelet.

"Kelly! Omigod! There it is! You found it!"

I held up the towel. The clasp of the bracelet was caught in a loop of the terry cloth. I looked at

Jennifer. Neither one of us could believe it. Very carefully I unhooked it from the towel and held out the bracelet in my hand for Jennifer to see.

Her mouth was still hanging open, this dopey grin on her face.

"You found it! I can't believe it! You actually found it!"

I closed my hand tight around the little chain of gold and smiled back at her.

"Yeah. I found it."

# CHAPTER 30

"That is the weirdest thing that I have ever seen in my entire life." Jennifer's eyes were locked on mine. She rubbed her hands across her arms and shivered. "It's like you're psychic! Are you psychic?"

I shook my head. I was still holding my closed fist up in the air. "I never was before."

"How did you do that? How did you know where to look?"

"I didn't. I just . . . all of a sudden . . . I don't know. Something reminded me of when we took her towel."

We both looked at Melissa's towels, all rumpled up now. It'd been stuck inside the towel at the bottom of the stack. I thought about how she probably did the same thing I did—used the same couple of towels all the time, and then when they came back clean from the laundry, she'd fold them and put them at the top of the stack. The ones at the bottom might not ever get used.

"If I didn't find it there, I was going to check the showers next. It was just luck. Just pure luck."

Jennifer shook her head in amazement. "I still can't believe it. Wait till you tell her. She'll be so happy."

"Yeah," I agreed. "But first . . . first, let's tell Reb about it."

We found Reb at the tennis courts. She was smashing serves across the net to Tis, like a shot out of a cannon. Her face was total concentration, and she didn't even see us at first. Jennifer stayed by the edge of the court, but I walked right across it, with complete disregard for proper etiquette.

When Reb saw me coming, she stopped in mid-serve.

"Come here. I've got something to show you." Then I walked off. I didn't look back. I just assumed she'd follow me.

"Ah, excuse me?" I heard Tis say.

"Sorry. Go ahead. Help Santana and Jessica," Reb yelled back at her.

I smiled. Reb was following me.

I walked over to the hill by the tennis courts overlooking the lake and sat down in the grass. Jennifer sat down beside me. Reb walked up to us, holding her racket. She stopped right in front of me.

She didn't look mad. She *did* look interested. But she didn't say a word.

"Look what I found." I held my hand out and opened it up.

Reb looked surprised. She stepped forward like she wanted to touch it, but then she stopped.

"Go ahead," I said. I held it out to her and she took it from me. She held it up between her fingers.

"We just found it. Five minutes ago."

"*You* found it," Jennifer corrected.

"Where?" Reb sounded curious. Very gently she handed the bracelet back to me.

"Folded up in Melissa's towel. The one we took . . . the one I took from the shower that day."

"Huh." Reb made a little surprised noise.

"Kelly is psychic. Reb, it was the freakiest thing. You should've been there. We were in the cabin—"

"I'm not psychic."

Reb's mouth twitched a little. Was that a smile? "You did find it, though."

"Yeah. And I'm really glad. But I also feel totally guilty."

"What for?" she asked. She was still standing there in front of Jennifer and me, holding her racket. I wished she'd sit down with us. I wanted to pat the grass next to me to make her sit down, but I didn't. The sun was behind her back, and her face was a shadow.

"Well, we kept telling her we didn't take it. But in a way we did. At least I did. If I hadn't stolen her towel, she never would've lost it. It was all my fault."

Reb gazed at the lake off in the distance. Was she still going to give me the silent treatment? Tell me to leave her alone? None of us said anything. Finally, Reb cleared her throat. "You mean—if I hadn't made you take her towel, she never would've lost it. So I guess it was all my fault."

"I'm not blaming you."

She glanced at me, then looked back at the lake. She was swatting her leg with her racket. "I know you're not."

There was another long pause. I didn't know what to say, and Jennifer didn't seem to either. Reb was so quiet. She didn't seem mad, though. She seemed to be in some kind of trance.

"I guess we should give it back to her," I said finally.

Reb nodded, but she kept looking at the lake.

"Will you guys come with me?" I asked softly.

"I'll pass," said Reb, still staring at the lake. I felt so disappointed—I'd hoped that maybe this would fix things somehow. But I guess I was wrong.

I looked at Jennifer. "How about you?"

Jennifer sighed. "I hope you don't mind, but . . . I think you should do it. You're the one who found it. And you're better friends with her."

"I was never really friends with her."

Jennifer put her head down on her knees. "Well, you were nicer to her than we were."

That wasn't saying much. *I never expected the Evil Twins to be nice, but I thought you were.* Maybe now I really could be the nice one.

I stood up and brushed the grass off the back of my shorts. I had to go find Melissa.

Riflery was her favorite activity, so I checked there first. And Melissa was there. This was my lucky day. There were about five or six girls lying on the mattresses on the platform, propped up on their elbows to shoot. But Melissa was sitting up. I watched them for a few minutes. Jamie, the riflery counselor, asked me if I wanted to shoot some targets, but I told her I was waiting for someone.

When the shooters were done, they all laid down their rifles and went to get their targets. Melissa was walking back, looking at her target, when I went up to her.

"How'd you do?"

"Oh, uh, pretty good." Melissa looked up at me, all surprised.

I glanced at the target. She'd hit three bull's-eyes and two bullets in the nine-point ring. That was forty-eight points out of fifty. "Wow! That's incredible! How come you sit up, though?"

"Oh. I passed that progression, so now I sit. The next position is standing."

"That's really good." It was so good, I couldn't believe it. I was really impressed.

"Aren't you going to shoot?" Melissa asked.

"Um, no. Actually, I came to see you. Look what I found." I reached in my shorts pocket and carefully took out her bracelet.

Melissa clutched her chest and gasped. *"My bracelet!"* Then she reached out for it. Her hands were shaking. "You *found* it! Oh, I can't believe it! I never thought I'd see it again! I've been hoping and praying. . . . Thank you! Thank you!"

"Well . . . don't thank me. It was my fault."

Melissa was trying to put it on her wrist, but it was kind of awkward because it's a one-handed motion, so I helped her with it. She looked at me, all curious. "What do you mean?"

"Um. Well. Remember that day we took your towel? I was the one who grabbed it. And that's where I found it. Inside your towel."

"Inside my towel?" Obviously Melissa wasn't really following me, but she looked like she didn't really care. She was so happy.

"Yeah. When I found it, it was actually stuck to the towel. The clasp was caught on it. I guess when I took your towel, the bracelet must've been lying on it. It got stuck to the towel. And then I put the towel back on your shelf. With the bracelet stuck to it."

Melissa nodded, like she was remembering. "Yeah. It *was* around that time when I lost it. I remember I was so mad about my towel and robe being taken, and then I couldn't find my bracelet, and I thought, 'What a terrible day!'"

"I didn't see the bracelet, Melissa. I swear I didn't. It was an accident. I really didn't mean to hide it from you. If I'd known where it was, I would've given it back to you sooner. I'm really sorry."

Melissa was smiling. She obviously didn't care. She

had her bracelet back and that was all that mattered.

"The funny thing is—it was with your stuff all along. You'd have found it eventually. At least when you got home and unpacked your trunk."

"Oh! I still can't believe it! I am *so* happy! It would have killed me if I'd lost it forever. It's so important to me."

"I know. I'm really sorry."

"Oh, it's back now! That's all I care about. Thanks, Kelly! Thank you so much."

"You're welcome."

She didn't hate me. I was a little surprised. She had every right to. I walked away, relieved that at least the missing bracelet was found. But I still felt bad. Melissa had put up with a lot. If all that stuff had happened to me, what would I have done?

I wasn't sure. I was glad I didn't have to find out.

# CHAPTER 31

"Boo!" Reb stepped out from behind a tree right in front of me, and I jumped. We were in the little patch of woods near the riflery range. She must have followed me, or maybe she was waiting for me. She was still carrying her tennis racket, and Jennifer was nowhere in sight.

We stood there looking at each other for a second.

"Did you give it back to her?"

"Yeah."

Reb nodded. "Did she blame you? You know, for the whole towel thing?"

"No, not at all. She was just so glad to get it back."

"I knew she would be."

We walked up the wooded path together. Neither

one of us said anything. I wondered if I should say something. Reb didn't seem like she was mad anymore. It was like the ice had thawed and she'd become unfrozen. She was just Reb again.

"You're a good person."

I stopped walking and looked at her. "What's that supposed to mean?"

Reb kind of smiled and didn't stop to wait for me. "It's not an insult. It's a compliment." She was walking ahead of me.

"Oh." I started walking again. "Thanks."

"I'm not." Long, long pause. "A good person, I mean."

I didn't know what to say to that. We were just walking along, not really looking at each other. "Sure you are."

"Not always."

"Well, nobody's a good person all the time," I said.

"True." Silence.

"It was just jokes. Just practical jokes. You know. Camp stuff. For fun. I mean, look at her. She's such a wimp. If you can't take a little heat at summer camp, you'll wilt in the real world."

I didn't say anything. Maybe I nodded a little.

"There's something about her that annoys me. She's

just so . . . *nerdy*. She's so quiet, it's like she's afraid of her own shadow."

"She's good at riflery, though. She just shot a forty-eight."

Reb shrugged. "Whatever. I guess everyone's good at *something*. Anyway, I thought I was doing her a favor. Toughening her up a little."

"I doubt she's any tougher now than when camp started," I said.

"Maybe not. I guess I didn't really do her any favors, huh?"

Then she didn't say anything for a long time. She walked along, swinging her racket.

Then all of a sudden, really abruptly, she said, "Are we friends again?"

"I hope so. I want to be."

"Are you still mad at me?" she asked. She was walking ahead of me, whacking away the branches on the path in front of us like she was clearing it with a machete or something. I felt like we were in a jungle.

"Reb, I was never mad at you. Are you still mad at me?"

She kept swinging her racket. Left, right, left, right. "Are you sure you don't hate me? Think you'll ever forgive me? Think you could lower yourself to be friends with me again?" she asked over her shoulder.

"I forgive you." Whack, whack, whack. "Do you forgive *me*?" I yelled at her. She was way up ahead of me now, far up the path. Walking faster and faster.

"Do you hate me?" she asked. It seemed like she was asking the trees.

"No."

"Do you like me again?"

"Yes," I answered. I almost said, *I never stopped liking you*, but I didn't. That's not how she wanted me to play the game.

"Can you lower yourself to be friends with me?" she asked the woods around us.

"Yeah, I can," I said out loud, to the trees. "I'll just have to lower myself."

## CHAPTER 32

## Friday, July 11

"I'll never take it off again. They'll bury me in it," Reb said solemnly, slipping the pink wristband over her hand.

"Oh, shut up! Stop making fun of me. I'm just so happy we're all triplets again," said Jennifer.

I was too. Good thing I didn't throw my wristband away in the woods, because now we were having a "banding ceremony," as Jennifer called it.

"And now for the wall signing." Jennifer pulled the cap off her Sharpie and handed it to Reb. Reb looked at the marker. "Am I supposed to say some sort of incantation first?"

Jennifer smacked her arm. "Shut up and sign."

Reb sucked on her lips to keep from smiling. "At

least you're not making me do it in blood." She wrote her name on a bare spot on the wall, then handed me the marker. I signed my name under hers; then Jennifer signed her name and wrote "Terrible Triplets" across the top. Next summer we could all come back to Cabin 1 and see where we'd signed our names.

"Good," said Jennifer. "Okay, now we can get ready for the Circle Fire." She went to her shelf and got a can of bug repellent. Pretty soon the whole cabin was engulfed in a stinky fog.

"Let me warn you guys in advance. I'm going to cry my eyes out. I do every year," said Jennifer.

"Some people actually cry?" I asked. Everybody had been talking about how sad the Circle Fire was going to be. I didn't really get it.

"Some people? Try everyone. Everyone cries," Jennifer told me.

"Even the counselors? Even Eda?" I asked. I dug through my trunk for my white Pine Haven polo. I'd never admit this to anyone, but I actually liked wearing the uniform—white polos with a green Pine Haven logo and white shorts. We only had to wear it on Sundays and special occasions, which wasn't too bad. And it made me feel like I was part of something. Just like the wristbands did.

"Some counselors cry. Eda never cries, but almost every single camper does," said Jennifer.

I looked at Reb. I couldn't imagine her crying. She was too cool. She must've read my mind, because she said, "It's not like all the other campfires. The Circle Fire's different. Everybody's all serious. It's the time to say good-bye."

Molly and Jordan walked in, and instead of going over to their side like they usually did, they came over and sat around on our side, and a few minutes later so did Erin and Brittany. We were all still talking about the talent show the night before.

"Good job, guys," said Reb. "Sorry we didn't help you out too much."

"Yeah, it was great. A lot better than if we'd been involved, I'm sure," said Jennifer. We did feel bad that all of us on Side A had dumped the talent show on the B girls, but they did a really great act. They dressed up like Tarzan and Jane and a couple of monkeys and did a dance routine. It was freaking hilarious. It ended up being one of the best acts.

"Thanks, guys," Molly said. "We owe it all to Jordan," which was kind of a joke, because Jordan got sick and had to go to the infirmary. She almost missed the whole thing. Poor Jordan. There was always something to stress her out.

The screen door banged and Melissa came in. When she saw us all sitting there, she froze for a second, like she didn't want to come in.

"Hey, what's up?" asked Molly.

"I was just going to get dressed," said Melissa. "What's happening with the CAs? Did anyone hear?" At least Melissa was trying to interact with the rest of us.

"I heard none of them are getting hired back next year," whispered Jordan.

"No way!" whispered Brittany. "That's so unfair!"

"I'm not sure that's true," said Erin. "I think everyone's saying that, but I doubt Eda will actually be that tough on them."

It was a huge deal. All the CAs, including Tis, had been caught in a prank against Camp Crockett, and the rumors were that they were in huge, huge trouble with Eda. We didn't even know what had happened for sure. Some people said they'd been caught at Camp Crockett late at night in the middle of the prank. Some people said they hadn't actually left Pine Haven yet, but were in a van on their way over there when Eda found out about it. None of us knew what had happened, and Tis would hardly say a word. She was obviously upset about it, but she wouldn't tell us what happened.

"That would suck so bad if they couldn't come back

next year," said Reb. "I'm coming back until I'm a counselor. I plan on working here every summer till I graduate from college."

We all said we wanted to come back next year too. Even Melissa chimed in and said *she* was coming back. I found *that* hard to believe. Maybe she said it because we were all saying it. Or maybe she really did want to come back.

Reb and Melissa didn't look at each other, of course. Ignoring each other was probably the best they'd ever do. At least it was better than open warfare.

All of a sudden, Rachel's face appeared, pressed up against the window screen. "Ah, look at my little chickadees! All here together. I can't believe you're all leaving the nest tomorrow. That makes me so sad!" Her face was scrunched up in a fake cry.

"Where's Tis? Are the CAs getting fired?" asked Jennifer.

Rachel came inside and plopped down on her bed. "They're not getting fired." She had on her green polo that the counselors wore.

"Are they going to get hired back next year?" asked Molly.

Rachel shrugged and didn't say anything. We could tell she didn't really want us to ask her about it. She kept changing the subject, talking to us about how we were going home tomorrow and asking if we had everything packed. And then it was time to go.

So all of us in Cabin 1 walked down to the Circle Fire together. It was just before dark, and the light was really soft and gray. We could see a few lightning bugs light up here and there above the grass. The Circle Fire was at Lakeview Rock. It was almost like a rock cliff that you could walk out on, and it was big enough for the whole camp to sit on. If you walked to the edge, you could stand there overlooking the lake.

By the time we got there, the big campfire was already lit and a bunch of campers were sitting down in a circle around it. We all sat down together. Gloria Mendoza, a counselor in Cabin 4, was softly playing one of Pine Haven's mellow songs on her guitar. The smell of wood smoke filled the air. I could feel the heat from the fire on my face, but the air on my back was nice and cool.

We started off singing songs, but none of the rowdy, loud songs that we sang in the dining hall during meals. We sang serious songs about sisterhood and friendship. Reb and Jennifer were right. Everyone was all quiet, and the mood was pretty solemn. It was like the fire hypnotized us. We were all just singing and staring into it, listening to it pop and crack.

People took turns standing up and giving speeches about what camp meant to them. Eda tried to balance things out by asking old campers and new campers to say something. A few counselors gave little speeches too.

I sat there and looked around at everyone. I couldn't believe that this was really our last night of camp. Tomorrow we'd all be going home. No wonder everyone cried at the Circle Fire. I had to come back next year. And the summer after that. That was the only way I could stand to leave tomorrow, if I knew that camp didn't have to end forever.

Now some of the counselors were opening up cardboard boxes and passing around little white candles to all of us. Then Eda stood up to give her speech. "Every summer since 1921, girls just like you have been coming to Pine Haven. And every summer when it's time to say good-bye, we have a Circle Fire. Good-byes are difficult, but they're necessary."

By that time pretty much everybody was crying. Some girls were just sniffling and looking red-eyed, but others were really sobbing. We all had our arms around each other's shoulders. Eda stuck a long wooden match into the fire to light it. Then she lit her candle and turned and lit the candle of the counselor standing next to her. Then the counselor passed the flame to the girl next to her, and we kept passing the flame around from one person to the next. Finally, after the flame had been passed all the way around, all our candles were lit.

"Every summer we all come together for one month, which always seems to fly by much faster than we want it to. While we're all together, we form a whole. We're the girls and young women of Pine Haven. It's that sense of togetherness that makes our camp such a special place. But tomorrow we'll leave Pine Haven to go back to our homes and families. The campfires will all be out here."

Then Libby, my old friend from Solitary, and another counselor picked up shovels and threw dirt onto the fire until all the flames were out. That made everything a lot darker, except for all our little candles.

"Tonight, on our last night at camp, I'd like you to think about what each of your flames has added to the fire at Pine Haven. And also think about what the fire at Pine Haven has added to each of your flames."

Then Eda stepped back, and we all just stood there, really quiet, holding our candles in front of our faces. With the whole camp there, we made a really big circle. You could see the flames flickering a little, and now with the fire out, the night air felt really cool. In the candlelight, everyone looked alike. We were all wearing our white polos and holding candles. It was strange that you sometimes couldn't even tell who was who. But I liked it. It was really pretty and nice.

Now we started to walk away from the campfire. We could walk around with our candles for a while before we went to the cabins. But we couldn't talk. That was the tradition. From now till tomorrow morning, we couldn't say anything. We had to respect the tradition and keep silent. As people walked away, all the lights from the candles bobbed up and down. Pretty soon you could see them all over the hill. I couldn't believe how beautiful the night looked, with all the little flames scattered all around. Down by the lake, you could see candles along the bank, and the lake itself looked like black glass.

I walked along with all the other Cabin 1 girls back up the hill, tilting my candle forward a little so the warm wax would drip in the grass instead of running down my arm. I was still sniffling. Jennifer was right. Everyone had cried. Even Reb got pretty teary toward the end. By the time we got up to the cabin, we blew out our candles and got undressed and into bed without turning on any lights.

Silent and dark and sad. That's how I'll always remember the last night.

CHAPTER 33

## Saturday, July 12

"I promise I'll e-mail all of you at least once," said Brittany. "But if you don't write me back, I won't keep bugging you, so . . ."

"I'd rather IM," said Molly. "Or text, except my parents refuse to buy me unlimited, so I have to pay for all my text messages."

That was pretty much the conversation at breakfast—what was the best way to keep in touch: by phone, e-mail, or some variation. I was just trying really hard not to puke. The smell of oatmeal and greasy link sausages didn't help any. Just thinking about the ride home in the car through those windy mountain roads made me queasy.

But once breakfast ended and we went outside, the

fresh air calmed my stomach a little. All the counselors were wearing their green Pine Haven polos and white shorts so they'd look official for the parents. The last day. Tonight I'd be sleeping in my own bed at home. I dreaded having to wait around for my parents to get here. I just wanted to snap my fingers and be home.

Everything was as bustling as it had been on the first day. A truck full of Camp Crockett counselors pulled up, and the guys hopped out to help move trunks and carry stuff. Already a few cars were driving up the gravel road. Pretty much the entire camp was standing around on the hill, waiting.

"I can't believe this is really happening," moaned Jennifer. "We're leaving. This is the end. Tomorrow we won't even see each other, and then the day after that . . ."

"Shut up, all right? We get it," Reb snapped at her. "It's bad enough. You're just making it worse."

The two of them were leaving for the Asheville airport at eleven o'clock. My parents had said in their last e-mail that they'd be here sometime in the middle of the morning, whatever that meant. I refused to look at my watch.

It was horrible. We said good-bye to Erin first, and some other people, and then some more people.

Somehow Brittany left and we didn't even get a chance to say good-bye to her. Then Rachel came and found us and said that Melissa was leaving.

"Don't you want to say something to her?" she asked us before walking off to greet Melissa's mom.

Jennifer looked at Reb and me. "How about, 'Sorry we ruined your life. Hope you don't turn psycho'?"

Reb tried not to smile. "What do you think, Kel? Should we say anything to her?" She was pretty much the same old Reb as before, except now she seemed to ask my opinion more than she used to.

"Wouldn't hurt to say good-bye," I suggested.

We walked over to Melissa's car. Tis and Rachel were giving her a hug, and Molly and Jordan were there too, telling her to have a good year and they hoped they'd see her next summer and blah, blah, blah.

Melissa got into her car and closed the door. She was probably glad to be leaving early. She saw me through the half-open window and smiled and waved. I noticed she was wearing her bracelet. I waved back and smiled too.

"Good-bye!" we all yelled as the car turned around in the gravel and drove away.

At least we'd said good-bye to her.

Jennifer shrugged. "Well, that wasn't so bad."

"No, but this is going to be." Reb pointed to a blue van where Eda stood with her clipboard. It was the eleven o'clock van to the Asheville airport. She was starting to call off names.

"God, this sucks. We've got to go," said Jennifer, on the verge of tears.

"I forgot something!" Reb said all of a sudden. "In the cabin—hang on a second!" She took off and was halfway up the hill before Jennifer and I even figured out what was going on.

Jennifer looked at me. "What's she doing? She couldn't have left anything. . . ."

"I know. She checked and rechecked everything about fifty times," I said. We started up the hill after her to see what she was up to, but she met us on the way down.

"It's all good," she assured us. And then she winked at me.

"What was it?" asked Jennifer.

"My Little Mermaid bra. I forgot to pack it."

Jennifer rolled her eyes. "Whatever."

When we got to the van, Jennifer and Reb were the last ones to get in. They said good-bye to Tis and Rachel and everybody else, and then they looked at me.

Reb grabbed the two of us. "Okay, let's not get

sappy. We know we'll keep in touch. And then next summer . . . it'll be the Terrible Triplets, same as always, right?"

Her voice was all hoarse. We touched wristbands, and for once Reb didn't roll her eyes. Then they both hugged me, and I was already jealous that the two of them at least got to ride together to Asheville, but I was going to be left all alone. Jennifer was sobbing. Reb's eyes were red. I had snot coming out of my nose. I wish I could cry more gracefully.

Then they got into the van and the doors were closed. I didn't stay to watch it drive away. I was running up the hill to the cabin. Everything was a blur of green.

I still needed to take my sheets off my bed and stuff them into my trunk. When I burst through the screen door and saw how empty everything was, that just made me cry harder. But then I stopped.

There was something on my pillow.

It was a shirt, all folded up in a neat square. And a piece of folded paper on top.

It was Reb's Abercrombie shirt—the one she'd loaned me for the first Camp Crockett dance. I picked up the sheet of Pine Haven stationery covered in Reb's neat handwriting.

Hey Kelly,

Sorry about the way things have been between us this week.

And about all the mean things I said to you. I think you've forgiven me, but I just wanted to let you know I was sorry. Anyway, we are friends. FOREVER. And don't you forget it.

                                                    Reb

P.S. It's not a kidney, but I wanted to give you something.

P.P.S. Triplets Rule!

I actually hugged the shirt. Not because it was an Abercrombie shirt either. I didn't even care about that. I took off my T-shirt and slipped Reb's shirt on. Then I pulled the sheets off my bed and crammed them into my trunk.

But the last thing I put in was Reb's note on top. That way when I opened up my trunk at home that evening, it'd be the first thing I saw.

Don't miss a single camper's story—here's a sneak peek at JD's, in *Summer Camp Secrets: Acting Out!*

## Sunday, June 15

This was it. I was about to leave my past behind me and start my new life. All I had to do was say good-bye to my family and get on the bus.

My mom clutched my arm. "Promise me you'll wear your headgear," she said, loud enough for twenty people to hear. Was that the most important thing she had to say to me before I left for a whole month?

"Mom! I told you I would. Stop asking me." We were in a huge crowd of parents and kids, all hugging and saying good-bye.

I looked around at the girls near me. One girl had on a ton of eye makeup, and she kept looking at her nails. They had that stupid white line painted across the top. The girl beside her was chatting away about something.

Another girl stood with her parents, not saying anything. She held a unicorn backpack in front of her like a shield.

"We'll e-mail you tomorrow to see how you're doing, but you'll have to write us back by snail mail, so I packed some envelopes and stamps for you," said Mom.

"Okay, thanks." I tried to sound grateful instead of annoyed, since she'd told me this three times already. She had her arm around me, and she wouldn't let go. It wasn't her fault she was being so clingy. This was my first time away from home.

"Gimme a hug, darlin'." Dad grabbed me away from Mom and squeezed my guts out. A couple of the other dads looked up at him. He's six foot four, so he's easy to spot in a crowd. "Have a great time. And don't worry about us. We can take care of ourselves."

I nodded but didn't say anything. I wished he hadn't said not to worry. How could I not? But maybe I'd have a break from worrying about my family for a while.

Then Adam hugged me. "Have fun, munchkin. Don't get eaten by a bear."

"I won't!" I laughed and hugged him back. He's fifteen, and he's already six foot one. I was going to miss being called munchkin. I felt small around my dad and brothers, but most of the time I felt like a giant freak, since I'm so tall for a girl. "Thanks for coming with us," I told him, but then I wished I hadn't said it. It made it sound like I was mad at Justin because he was still in bed when we left. I'd had to say good-bye to him at home.

"I guess I should go," I said. The bus engine was rumbling, and stinky gas fumes filled up the whole parking lot. Mom hugged me one more time and then finally let me go so I could get in line. I looked at the sign on the front of the bus. CAMP PINE HAVEN. Cool. My new life was about to begin.

I stood in line, smushed between girls in front of me and behind me. I kept my tennis racket pointed down so I wouldn't bop anyone in the knees. Somehow the girl with the unicorn backpack had ended up in front of me, only now the backpack was on her shoulders and pressed against my stomach.

I looked back at my family and waved before going up the steps. Mom smiled but she was blinking a lot, so I knew she was about to cry. Dad and Adam waved back.

We all shuffled down the bus aisle. Girls were cramming pillows, backpacks, and other junk in the overhead storage bins and holding up the whole line. By the time I made it halfway down the aisle, all the front seats were full. So what? I wanted to sit in the back anyway. I walked past the eye makeup girl and her friend, past the unicorn backpack, and was about to sit next to a girl with a long brown ponytail when she stuck her hand over the empty space and said, "It's taken."

The girl in the seat behind Ponytail said, "You can sit here."

"Thanks." I shoved my tennis racket and backpack in the overhead bin and plopped down in the seat next to her. She smiled at me. She was African American, and she had on little wire-rimmed glasses, a yellow tank top, and daisy earrings. She was really tiny. She probably didn't weigh more than seventy pounds dripping wet with rocks in her pockets.

"I'm Natasha."

"Hi," I said. She glanced at me like she was waiting for something. The bus was moving now, and the driver was trying not to mow down all the parents still standing in the parking lot.

"What's your name?" she asked finally.

That was an easy question. Ordinarily. Most people know the answer to that by the time they're two. I almost gave her the wrong name, out of habit. But then I remembered who I was supposed to be.

"JD. That's what everyone calls me," I heard myself saying.

It felt so strange to say my new name out loud. Now that I'd told one person, there was no turning back. I'd have to stick to my plan.

"Nice to meet you, JD." She cleared her throat. I could tell she was a little on the shy side, but I still liked her. "What does JD stand for?"

I stared at her like I was in a trance. What was I supposed to say to that? I thought I could just tell people to call me JD and they would. Did they have to know my whole boring life story?

I tried to think of something funny. "Just Dandy!" I said. It wasn't that funny, but it was better than the truth. Natasha looked at me like I was speaking Portuguese.

"Okay, I'm kidding. That's not what it stands for." I stalled, trying to think of a better answer. The bus made a wide turn and I gripped the seat in front of me to keep from sliding over and smashing Natasha against the window.

"You want to know what it really stands for? It's pretty embarrassing."

Natasha's eyes got bigger. "Oh, you don't have to tell me."

"No, I don't mind. My first name is January and my middle name is December. Crazy, huh? I have really weird parents. You know, the New Agey type. It could've been worse. At least they didn't name me Apple."

Natasha smiled, which made me feel bad about telling her such a goofy story. But it was part of the plan. I wanted to make sure no one at camp ever knew my real name.

Judith Duckworth. I've always hated my name. It thounds like I'm lithping when I thay it. Mom named me after her grandmother. She was crazy about her grandmother, and she thought naming me after her would be a great way to honor her. Too bad my great-grandma's name wasn't Ashley.

I'd never told anyone to call me JD before, but that was about to change. I'd tried to come up with some kind of nickname for myself, but I didn't want Judy—that sounded old to me—and Ducky was even worse. I figured initials would be pretty good. And I liked the way they sounded. JD. That was *sooo* much better than Judith. Already my life was improving.

Natasha looked at me. "Are you nervous about going to camp?"

"No. Why should I be? I think it'll be fun."

She smiled and scooted her glasses up on her nose.

"You're braver than I am. I'm nervous about meeting a lot of new people."

"You know what my dad said about going someplace where nobody knows you? He said I should think of it as a fresh start."

Natasha nodded like that made a lot of sense. My dad also said camp would give me a break from all the stuff our family has been through, but I didn't mention that.

A fresh start. That was what I was most looking forward to. Going someplace where nobody knew me.

Fifth grade was when I first realized how boring I was. That was the year Chloe Carlson came to our school. You'd think being the new girl would be hard, but it wasn't for this girl. From Day One all the boys were in love with her and all the girls wanted to be her friend. Part of it was her name. How could you be anything but cool with a name like Chloe Carlson? Her parents obviously knew what they were doing. They didn't name her something random like Bernice. Or Judith.

This year, in sixth grade, I tried to act like Chloe. I made funny comments in class and I tried to be everyone's friend, but it didn't really work. Everybody stared at me and said, "Why are you acting so weird?"

So when my dad said camp would be a fresh start, I figured it was time for a personality makeover. Then I had this great idea. I'd borrow Chloe's personality while I was away at this summer camp in North Carolina, and she'd never even have to know.

While I talked to Natasha, I tried to think what Chloe would do if she was on this bus right now. She'd say something funny loud enough for everyone to hear. I just wasn't sure what that funny thing would be.

"Do you have any brothers or sisters?" asked Natasha. Now the bus was making a humming noise, and everyone was pretty quiet, talking to the people next to them.

I thought about it for a second. I could tell her anything—make up an older sister or a baby brother. But I decided to go with the truth. I didn't want to act like Justin and Adam didn't exist. "Yeah. Two brothers. Both older. What about you?" At least I could tell her that and she wouldn't say, *Oh the football stars at Central High? THEY'RE your brothers?*

"I'm an only child."

"Really? What's that like?"

Natasha shrugged. "Okay, I guess. It's all I know. I think that's why my parents are sending me to camp. So I can see what it's like to live with other kids for a change. But I'm really going to miss them. The three of us are very close."

"Hey, we've got a whole month without parents," I said. "It'll be great." Then I did the craziest thing I've ever done in my life. I stood up and yelled really loud, "Hey, everyone, let's hear it for a whole month without parents!" Then I whooped, the way I would at Justin's and Adam's football games. "Woo-hoo! Woo-hoo!"

When everyone turned and stared at me, I smiled and waved, like I was glad to be making a fool of myself. Then I slid back down in the seat. Natasha's eyebrows were way above the rims of her glasses.

"Sorry. Didn't mean to cause a scene," I told her. I could tell she hadn't expected me to do that. *I* hadn't even expected me to do that. Chloe wouldn't have done something *that* stupid. I hoped I wasn't blushing. It felt weird being the center of attention—like I was wearing someone else's shoes instead of mine. It didn't seem to fit right.

"It's just that this bus ride is pretty boring, don't you think?" I asked Natasha, acting like I was used to being the life of the party. "I mean, look at everyone. They're all half-asleep. We should liven this place up. I know! Let's sing 'A Hundred Bottles of Beer on the Wall'! Everyone loves that song!" Maybe the more I acted this way, the faster I'd get used to my new self.

"No, they don't," said the ponytail girl in the seat in

front of us. "Why don't you do us all a favor and shut up?" she added over the back of her seat. The friend she'd saved a seat for turned around and gave me a dirty look too.

I had no idea what to say to that. For one thing, nobody would ever tell Chloe Carlson to shut up while she was being funny. And if anyone ever said anything slightly sarcastic to her, she always had a quick comeback. Always. I tried to think of something, but my brain was frozen.

The ponytail girl had turned back around. She figured she'd shut me up for good. I did feel pretty silly. I wasn't very good at acting this way. I felt like covering my face with my hands, so I did, but then I got inspired.

I sat there with my face covered up and pretended to cry. I let out these loud *boo-hoo* sounds. "I don't have any friends!" I sobbed, loud enough for everyone around me to hear. Then I looked up at Natasha. "Will you be my friend if I pay you a buck?"

That's when the girls behind me started to laugh. "I'll be your friend for five bucks!" somebody yelled.

"Twenty for me!"

Natasha shook her head and grinned. "I had no idea I was inviting a crazy person to sit beside me. JD, of course I'll be your friend, and you don't need to pay me a dollar." She looked over the back of the seat. "I'll do it for free!" she said.

"My first friend!" I yelled. "I actually have a friend now!" The two girls in front of us had put their pillows over the tops of their heads to cover up their ears. "And I've got some enemies, too!" I shouted.

Natasha cracked up laughing. I could only imagine what my friends back home would've said. *Judith, what's wrong with you? You never act like this.*

Maybe Judith didn't. But JD did.

"We're finally here!" said Natasha when we turned onto a gravel road and passed a sign that said CAMP PINE HAVEN FOR GIRLS. She jiggled her knee up and down as she looked out the window. We passed a lake and some tennis courts. There were tons of people all around and a lot of cars lined up along the road.

When we got off the bus, a bunch of counselors were waiting for us and yelling directions. They all had on matching green shirts, so they were easy to spot. They broke us up into age groups, and Natasha and I found out we were both in the group called Middlers—ages ten to twelve. That made us the oldest in the group.

Then a lady with a clipboard asked us our names. When it was my turn, I said, "JD Duckworth," like I'd always been called that. She looked at her list and didn't seem at all confused. "Okay, JD. You're in Middler Cabin Two A."

Then Natasha said, "Natasha Cox."

"Hi, Natasha. You're in Middler Cabin Three B."

Natasha and I looked at each other. "Can't we switch? We're best friends. We really need to be together," I said.

The lady shook her head. "Sorry, cabin assignments have already been made. But you'll still see a lot of each other." She smiled and moved on to the next girl.

Natasha and I walked over to where all the luggage from the bus was piled up. "I can't believe it. We just get to know each other and we're already split up," I said.

Natasha pushed her glasses up her nose. Now that I was standing next to her, I saw that she only came up to my shoulder. "I know, but like she said, we'll still see each other a lot."

Some guys wearing red T-shirts that said "Camp Crockett" helped us carry our trunks to the cabins. It was weird that the camp made everyone bring trunks to keep all their stuff in, but that's what the letter had said to do. Plus they gave us a list of what to bring and told us to put name tags in all our clothes. When my mom was getting my things ready, I felt like I'd joined the army.

We had to climb up a big hill to get to where the cabins were. I was glad I only had to carry my tennis racket and backpack.

"It sure is pretty here, isn't it?" asked Natasha. It was a sunny day, and everything was so green. There were trees everywhere, big rock formations, lots of hills, and off in the distance, bluish-colored mountains. All the buildings were wooden, and the whole camp looked like it should be on a postcard or something.

At the top of the hill we came to a long row of cabins. "Well, I guess this is good-bye—for now," said Natasha when we got to the door of Cabin 2. She looked scared.

"Okay. I'll see you later." It was too bad we couldn't stay together.

The guys carried my trunk in and left it inside. When I walked in, a counselor with curly blond hair said, "Hey! Are you my camper? I'm Michelle!"

She was obviously a counselor because she looked older, and she was wearing one of those green shirts, but I was about three inches taller than she was. I'm five foot six, and my doctor says I'm still growing. If I keep growing till I'm eighteen, I figure I'll be six-nine eventually.

"I'm JD. JD Duckworth."

She frowned a little like she'd never heard of me, but then she said, "Oh, okay. Nice to meet you, JD!" She had a great grin that made her eyes crinkle up.

The cabin was awesome. It had screens all around it, so it felt really open and breezy. And there were bunk beds. I've always wanted bunk beds. Justin and Adam had them a long time ago, but they each have their own room now.

"This is cool," I said, looking around at everything. The walls and floors were wooden, and girls had written their names all over the place.

"Wow! 1981!" I yelled. I pointed to a spot on the wall that said JENNIFER H. 1981. "That is so amazing! These cabins are that old?"

Michelle laughed. "Yeah. And guess what? My mom went here when she was a kid. And some people have grandmothers who went here. Can you believe it?" Her eyes crinkled again. "I'll send my daughter here too—if I have one."

Two other girls were already in the cabin, and while we were all trying to get everyone's names straight, another girl came in.

"Here. These will help us get to know each other faster," said Michelle. She handed out name tags. They were made out of little round slices of wood with a plastic string, but when I saw mine, I almost had a heart attack. It had JUDITH written on it. So much for keeping my old name a secret.

I held it against my stomach. "I need a new one. One that says 'JD.'"

"No problem! I'll just change the old one." Michelle took a marker from a shelf beside her bed and wrote "JD" in big red letters on the back of the piece of wood. Then she hung the string around my neck with the "JD" side showing. "How's that?"

"Good. But can I see the marker for a second?" I asked. I took off my name tag, scribbled over JUDITH so no one could read it, and then put it back on again.

All the other girls were watching me, but I didn't care. I was officially JD now.